The Weathermakers

D1191872

The Weathermakers

by BEN BOVA

HOLT, RINEHART AND WINSTON

New York   Chicago   San Francisco

Copyright © 1966, 1967 by Ben Bova.
All rights reserved, including the right to reproduce
this book or portions thereof in any form.
Published simultaneously in Canada by Holt, Rinehart
and Winston of Canada, Limited.

Library of Congress Catalog Card Number: 68–10078

Printed in the United States of America
SNB: 03–062385–5

Published, October, 1967

Second Printing, April, 1969

Portions of this book have appeared
in the December 1966 issue
of Analog.

To the President who accepted challenges "not because they are easy, but because they are hard," and who focused science and government on a difficult goal "because that challenge is one we are willing to accept, one we are unwilling to postpone, and one which we intend to win. . . ."

Preface

SINCE at least the time of Noah, the weather has been a major concern to man. Although scientists are now beginning to work toward weather modification and control, this book is not intended to be a prediction of how or when weather control will eventually come about. It is merely a story about people and ideas, and the way they sometimes interact.

Much of the science in this book has not been invented yet, and perhaps never will be. Science fiction assumes a poetic license that includes the right to use any idea—real or imagined—as long as it has not been proved to be wrong. I have tried to get the most accurate and up-to-date meteorological information for use in this story, and I am deeply indebted to meteorologist Robert C. Copeland for his help. The factual background of the story comes mainly from him. He is not responsible, though, for any bending of the facts or for the not-yet-invented science that appears in the story. I have tried to make the imaginary science at least plausible, and not completely beyond the realm of actual possibility.

Many others have added technical information and useful ideas to this book. If I tried to list them all, I would surely forget a few names. Therefore I thank them all equally, and hope they forgive me for not naming them individually.

The editors at Holt, Rinehart and Winston—especially Ann Durell—have been tremendously helpful all through the genesis of this book. They encouraged the idea of "here and now" science fiction, spotted the flaws and inconsistencies that always crop up in a long story, and were gentle but firm about keeping the book to a reasonable length.

Finally, I must make my deepest bow to my wife, Rosa. She not only took time out from her own writing to type the draft manuscript, but she offered invaluable advice and assistance in thrashing out many points of the story. All this while raising our children and keeping house. What's more, she even began complaining, when the weather turned sour, that there ought to be a Ted Marrett somewhere, hard at work.

Arlington, Massachusetts
December 1966

Contents

The Weathermakers

1. The First Day

∧∧∧∧∧∧∧∧∧∧∧∧∧∧∧∧∧∧∧

THE day I first met Ted Marrett began on Oahu. I had finished school in February, and Father had given me a desk and a title at his Thornton Pacific Enterprises, Inc. But I preferred the beach.

My three brothers and I always rose early, Father saw to that. But that morning, when they went to the office, I ducked out for surfing.

The tide was right, the surf booming, the sky bright and nearly cloudless. Nobody else was on the beach this early in the day, although I knew some of my beach pals would start to show up a little later. After a half hour of riding the big ones, a sectioning wave wiped me off the board, and down I went, gasping and struggling while tons of foaming water poured over me. I got out okay, dragged my board back onto the sand, and stretched out in the early sun to watch perfect twelve-footers curl in.

After a few minutes I started to get bored, so I reached out and turned on the portable TV I had brought with me. There was a western on; I had seen it before, but it wasn't too bad.

ELTING MEMORIAL LIBRARY
93 MAIN STREET
NEW PALTZ, N. Y.

The pocketphone in my beach robe buzzed. I knew who it would be. Sure enough, when I pulled the phone out and flicked it on, Father's face appeared on the tiny screen, looking as ominous as the thunderheads that pile up on the windward slopes of the island's mountains.

"If you can tear yourself away from the beach, I need you here at the office."

"Need me?"

He almost smiled at my surprise. "That's right. Your brothers can't handle everything for me. Get down here right away."

"Can't it wait 'til lunch? Some of the crowd will be coming along and we—"

"Now," he said, "if you don't mind."

When Father used that tone of voice, with that expression on his face, you didn't discuss the matter any further. I left the surfboard and TV for the beach boys to pick up and went back to the house. After a quick shower and change I dialed for a car. In five minutes I was cruising down the private road from our beach house to the main highway. I set the car on automatic; not that there was any traffic to cope with, I just wanted to see the rest of that western.

I was too late. The movie was finished and the news was on. Another storm had hit the Thornton mid-Pacific mining dredges, the news commentator said cheerfully, and a couple of men were missing. "All but two of the six-hundred-man team of engineers and technicians are safe," was the way he put it. That explained the expression on Father's face.

But what did he expect me to do about it?

A few minutes on the electronically controlled highway

and the car was at the Thornton Pacific Enterprises building. As I walked into Father's spacious, thickly carpeted office, he was standing by the windowall, moodily staring out at the sparkling ocean. He turned and looked at me in that pained way of his.

"At least you could have worn something decent."

"But you're wearing shorts too," I said.

"This is a business suit," he said, "not a walking flower garden."

"I just took the first things I found in the closet. You said to hurry."

"You were *supposed* to be here at the office, not at the beach."

I must have made a sour face.

"Jeremy, this is your business just as much as it is mine and your brothers'. I don't see why you can't take an interest in it. Your brothers—"

"There's nothing for me to do here, Dad. Nothing interesting, anyway. You're running things fine without me."

"Nothing interesting?" He looked amazed and angry at the same time. "Running the world's first deep-sea mining operation, not interesting? Operating intercontinental rocket transports, not interesting?"

I shrugged. "It's routine, Dad. You've done all the new work, the hard work. You and Rick and all. There's nothing new in it any more; no kicks in it, not for me."

Father shook his head unbelievingly. "Your brothers started out exactly where you are today, but they sank their teeth into their work and helped me to build up Thornton Pacific. I expect you to do the same. Don't fail me, Jeremy."

I didn't answer.

He went to his desk and glanced at a sheet of notes.

"Well, I've got a job for you, interesting or not. You're going to Boston on the ten o'clock flight, which means you'll have to hurry to catch the rocket."

"Boston? To see Uncle—"

"This is a business flight, not a social call. You're going to the Climatology Division. You'll be in New York by four thirty Eastern Time, and you can get to Boston by five thirty at the latest. I'll have word sent to the Climatology people and tell them to expect you."

"Who's the Climatology Division? What's this all about?"

"The storms, what else?" he snapped. "Climatology's part of the Weather Bureau—the part that makes long-range forecasts and handles weather modifications."

"Oh. I heard about the storms on the way in. Any further word about the missing men?"

"Not yet," Father said, sitting down in his contoured desk chair. "They were caught in the tethered pressure chamber when the storm hit. The cable snapped. The chamber must be at the bottom, but we can't find it."

"How deep is it where they went down?"

"Eighteen thousand feet. We've recovered men from worse spots, but that's deep enough. One of them has been with me since I started in business here. If we lose them. . . ."

"They'll be all right for twelve hours in the chamber, won't they?"

"If it stays intact." He slammed a fist against the desk top. "These blasted storms! This is the third one in ten days, and April's not half over yet. If the weather out there doesn't improve we'll have to shut down altogether. The contract with Modern Metals will be defaulted. We could lose millions!"

"Is it really that bad?"

"I've been in this business as long as anyone, Jeremy," he said, nodding toward the model of CUSS V, which drilled the original Mohole. "This is the stormiest spring I've ever seen. The Climatology people have got to help us. I could talk to them on the phone, but personal contact always gets better results. Now, you find the man in charge of weather modification and don't let go of him until he agrees to help us. Understand?"

Father's secretary had a travelkit for me, tickets for the rocket, and a helicab waiting on the roof to take me to the launch pad out in the harbor.

I was to travel on a Thornton Aerospace Corporation rocket, of course. The company was owned by Uncle Lowell, back in New England, but Father ran the Pacific end of it. Father had his differences with the rest of the Thorn family, but that never stood in the way of business. When Uncle Lowell had needed help in starting a commercial rocket transport line, Father had invested heavily. Naturally, Father's decision was influenced by the fact that his business interests spanned the broad Pacific, and rocket transports could haul the ore dredged from the sea bottom to the industrial heartland of America in half an hour.

The rocket wasn't tall and sleek, like those used for space flights. It was squat and heavy-looking, with its reusable propellant tanks clustered around the main body. Nearly two hundred passengers were filing into the four-decked cabin as my helicab approached the landing barge. Across the harbor I could see the U.S.S. *Arizona* memorial, and farther in the distance a tug was towing in empty rocket-booster stages from the impact area.

I was the last passenger aboard. There were guides and hostesses at every turn to cheer me across the access ramp, up the elevator, into the cabin, and onto one of the contoured couches.

Rocket travel was still new enough for there to be plenty of people who preferred "safe and conventional" supersonic jets to the "new and dangerous" global rockets. Even though the rockets were cheaper, enormously faster, and actually safer than jets! I remembered asking Father how people could be so dim-witted.

"There's a big difference between what engineers can do," he had answered, "and what people are willing to accept. It takes time for the average man's attitudes to adjust to a new idea . . . even if the idea will save him time and money."

I remember Father saying that very clearly, because the next four years of my life were spent living with exactly that problem.

The rocket flight was really uneventful: some pressure and noise at lift-off, a few shudders when they dropped the empty booster stages, a long floating weightless glide, and then more pressure squeezing me into the couch as we re-entered. There were no viewports in the passenger cabin, but you could see TV pictures of the world outside on the videoscreen over your couch. The people around me gaped at a color view of Earth, curving blue and flecked with dazzling white clouds; or at views of the stars or the moon. Some of them even claimed to see the pinpoint of light where Moonbase was located.

I had seen it before, so I watched the TV movies.

The outside cameras shut off when re-entry started. No sense startling the passengers with pictures of red-hot air engulfing the ship! As the detective movie on my screen ended, I heard the muffled roar of the retrorockets, and we settled on the special pad at the airfield.

It was warm and sticky outside. One of the Thornton Aerospace reservation clerks pushed through the crowd at the base of the rocket and handed me a tape spool. A message from Father. I thanked him and asked directions for the New York-Boston train. He ushered me to the proper slideway.

As I stepped on the moving belt that ran into the distant terminal building, I took out my pocketphone and snapped the tape into its spool holder. With the earplug in place, I could hear Father telling me:

"Jeremy, we've discovered the name of the man you should talk to at Climatology. His name is Rossman . . . he may be a Ph.D. Call him 'Doctor' anyway, he'll be flattered. He's in charge of the long-range predictions and weather-control work. We've set up a five-thirty appointment for you. Oh, by the way, the Navy found our two missing divers. They're pretty battered, but they'll pull through. Call me after you've seen Rossman. Good luck."

I stuffed the phone back in my shirt pocket and looked at my wristwatch. It said 10:38. Still on Hawaiian time. There wasn't a clock in sight as I whisked along toward the terminal building. All I could see was the bustling airport, with jets circling overhead and the rocket pad behind me. Far off in the distance was the vague blur of the Manhattan Dome that covered downtown New York City, its geodesic framework barely visible through the murky city smog.

The belt slid through the blast of air that curtained the

terminal doorway, and I spotted a clock—4:40 local time. I dashed down to the train tube level and caught a Boston express.

The pneumatic trains are fast and easy-riding, but the shriek of metal wheels on metal tracks at four hundred miles an hour is still terrible, no matter how much acoustical insulation they put in. I sat in a four-place compartment, alone, wondering if I could make my appointment on time.

It was exactly 5:20 when I stepped out of the train and into an elevator that took me to the top of the Transportation Tower in Boston's Back Bay. But it took the helicab driver nearly twenty minutes—and several dollars extra on the meter—to find the Climatology Department building, out in the suburbs.

The parking lot where the cab deposited me was nearly empty, and the lobby of the main building deserted except for a solitary uniformed guard sitting at the reception desk.

I walked across the polished lobby floor, feeling slightly foolish. "I'd like to see Dr. Rossman, please."

The guard looked up from his baseball magazine. "Rossman? He's left by now."

"But . . . but he's expecting me." I fumbled in my wallet and pulled out one of the business cards that Father had insisted on having printed for me.

"Well, I'm pretty sure he's gone. Wait a minute and I'll check."

He punched out a number on the desk intercom. It had no viewscreen, I noticed.

"Long-range," a strong voice answered.

"Is Dr. Rossman still there?"

"Yeah, he's waiting for some visitor . . . somebody named Thornton or something."

The guard looked at my card. "Jeremy Thorn the Third? From Thornton Pacific Enterprises?"

"That's him. Send him up."

The guard gave me directions. Up the stairs, down a corridor, past three cross-corridors . . . or was it four? After a few false turns and some headscratching, I heard that same telephone voice still going strong in conversation with someone else. Following the voice, I came to a door marked Long-Range Forecasts Section. All the other offices seemed to be empty.

I stepped through the open doorway and found myself in a sort of anteroom that housed secretaries' desks and file cabinets. A short hallway opened off the opposite side of the room, with several doors along the side. One door was ajar, and that was where the conversation was coming from.

I looked inside. It was a drab little cubicle. An elderly gentleman was sitting behind a desk buried under stacks of papers, while the person I had heard on the phone—tall, athletic-looking—was pacing before the chalkboard, his back to me. He was saying excitedly:

". . . and this paper by Sladek wraps it up. The Kraichnan Institute studies have paid off. You can predict what's happening in a turbulent flow without any trouble now."

The old man nodded gently. "Very nice, if true. But perhaps you can stop for a second and greet our visitor."

He whirled around. "Found us! Beginning to think we'd have to send out a search party."

"I nearly got lost," I admitted.

"Ted Marrett," he introduced himself, grabbing my hand

and pumping it hard. Gesturing, he added, "Dr. Barneveldt, chief of the theoretical section."

Ted was about my own age, perhaps a year or two older. He was big, heavy in the shoulders, flat in the midsection, with long, lanky legs. His face was bony, angular, and there was a barely visible scar across the bridge of his nose—a football injury, I learned later. His hair was an unruly mop of fire red. He hardly looked like a scientist who would shake the world.

While Ted was restless, gesturing, Dr. Barneveldt was small and quiet—almost sedate, in comparison. He was thin and slightly stoop-shouldered; his hair was dead white, and he had a somehow fragile look about him. The wrinkles on his face, though, seemed to come more from the little smile he constantly wore than from advancing age.

"Pleased to meet you both," I said. "I'm—"

"Jeremy Thorn the Third," Ted finished before I could. "Never met a Third before . . . or a Second, for that matter. Rocket in from Hawaii? Good flight? Sure dressed Island style."

"I . . . didn't have time to change," I fumbled. "Uh, is Dr. Rossman here? I was supposed . . ."

Ted nodded. "Told him you were here. He'll make you wait a couple minutes more before he lets you into his office. His way of getting even for making him wait."

"Getting even?"

"Quitting time's four fifteen around here; Rossman likes to get home to his wife and family. He was kind of sore about having to stay to five thirty, and you even blew *that* time."

"The helicab. . . ."

"Don't worry, he'll call you in any minute now."

I didn't know what to say. "You weren't staying late just because of me, were you?"

"Oh, no." Ted waved the idea away. Grinning toward Dr. Barneveldt, he said, "We were just gassing about weather control."

2. "... It's Impossible"

"WEATHER control?" I said. "That's what I came for."

"I believe perhaps we should explain," Dr. Barneveldt began to say, but a buzzer cut him off in mid-sentence.

He carefully moved a stack of paper off the desktop intercom and touched a red-glowing button.

"Has the visitor found the office yet?" a raspy voice asked.

"Yes," Dr. Barneveldt said. "Mr. Thorn is here now."

"Good; send him in." The intercom clicked into silence.

Ted gestured the old man to stay in his chair. "It's just down the hall," he said to me, jerking a thumb in the right direction. With the beginnings of a grin, he added, "Good luck."

I walked down the short hallway to the door at the end, feeling kind of jittery. There was no nameplate. I knocked once, lightly.

"Come in."

Dr. Rossman's office was almost as small and tired-looking as the one I had just left. A metal desk, a row of file cabinets, a tiny conference table with chairs that didn't match: no more furniture than that. Only one window; the rest of the walls were covered with charts and graphs that had been taped up years ago, from the looks of them.

I had never before realized the difference between private industry and government, as far as floor space and trappings were concerned. If Dr. Rossman had been working for Father at an equally important position, his office would have been four times larger. And probably his salary, too.

He was seated at the desk. "Sit down, Mr. Thorn. I hope you didn't have too much trouble finding us."

"A little," I answered. "I'm sorry if I've kept you late."

He shrugged. He was lean and pale-looking, with a long, somber face that reminded me a bit of a bloodhound's.

"Well, now," he said as I pulled a chair from the table toward the desk, "what can we do for Thornton Pacific?"

I sat down and said, "It's about these storms that have hit our mining dredges. They're causing a lot of damage and expense."

He nodded gravely. "Yes, I suppose they are."

"My father wants to know what you can do about them. We've been forced to suspend mining operations for several days at a time. If something isn't done soon to stop the storms, we're going to lose a considerable amount of money. To say nothing of the lives of the men who are in danger."

"I understand," Dr. Rossman said. "We've been trying to furnish the entire Pacific area with the most accurate long-range forecasts possible. Fully a third of my entire staff is working on the problem right now. Unfortunately, pinpointing storm development in the open ocean is a very, *very* difficult task."

"I guess it is."

"You see, Mr. Thorn, our long-range forecasts are made on a statistical basis. We can predict, with very good accuracy, how much rain will fall over a certain area during a given period of time—say, a month. But we can't foretell exactly when a storm will form until practically the last minute. And it's even more difficult to forecast a storm's exact path, except in a very general manner."

"Yes, but when a storm's going to affect a vital area such as our dredges," I asked, "can't you turn it aside or perhaps destroy it altogether?"

He nearly laughed, but checked himself just in time. "Mr. Thorn, whatever gave you the idea we could do that?"

"Well . . . aren't you the people who do the weather-control work? I've seen stories about cloud seeding and hurricane patrols. . . ."

"You're making a very common mistake," he said, smiling patiently. "Yes, my group here has the responsibility for weather modification *experiments*. The Weather Bureau has been doing small-scale seeding trials and other experiments for years. But they've never amounted to anything. Nothing definite has been proven. No one can alter the course of a storm. No one can dissipate a storm."

I could feel myself sink in the chair. "But those people who fly into hurricanes . . ."

"Oh, that. Yes, for years they've tried to modify hurricanes. But there's never been a firm connection established between what they do and the effect—if any—on the hurricane. *Never* has a hurricane been stopped, or even slowed down for long, as a result of seeding its clouds."

Leaning back in his swivel chair, he almost seemed to

be enjoying himself. "There's the Severe Weather group in Kansas City who've claimed they've prevented tornadoes —sometimes—by cloud seeding. But I'm not convinced, and neither is anyone else of any technical stature in the Weather Bureau. The results are far from conclusive."

I must have looked rather dumbfounded.

"Look at it this way," Dr. Rossman said, absently picking up a pencil from his desk. "A hurricane will expend within a few minutes as much energy as the Hiroshima A-bomb. In a single day, it will release the equivalent of a hundred ten-megaton hydrogen bombs. No one and nothing can destroy that!"

"But . . . smaller storms: can't you do something about them? Or at least try?"

He shook his head. "It would be enormously expensive, and completely futile, as far as I can see. In fact, hurricanes are probably more susceptible to man-made modifications than any other type of storm—at least, they seem more delicately balanced, closer to instabilities."

"That sounds strange."

"Yes," he agreed. "I suppose it does, to a layman. But it's true. As far as talk about controlling the weather, though, I'm afraid that's all it is—just talk. And I can assure you, no one from the Long-Range Forecasts Section will ever be involved in such foolishness as long as I'm in charge."

"Foolishness?"

"Of course it's foolishness," he snapped, waving the pencil at me. "Weather control! All the experiments we've done have been meaningless. Even supposing we *could* alter large-scale features of the weather . . . divert one of the storms that's been bothering you, or destroy it altogether. How do we know that we haven't created a condition where an even worse storm will develop? Or perhaps caused some changes in the natural balance of forces that will cause trouble thousands of miles away. No, there's too much involved, too much that we don't understand and probably never will understand. Believe me, as far as weather control is concerned . . . it's impossible."

"But those people in the other office—they were talking about weather control."

Rossman tried to smile again, but his eyes narrowed. "That's Ted Marrett. As I just explained to you, there's always a lot of *talk* about controlling the weather. Mr. Marrett is young and ambitious—going for his master's degree at MIT and all fired up, the world-beater type. I'm sure you've met his kind before. He'll settle down someday, and then he'll probably make a very fine meteorologist."

"Then . . . then there's nothing you can do to help us?"

"I didn't say that." Rossman tapped the pencil against his chin for a moment. "We can provide you with realtime service on our forecasts, for one thing. In layman's terms, that means we can furnish you with our forecasts by computer link as quickly as they're printed out here. I assume you're getting your forecasts now by commercial videophone, which is twelve to eighteen hours behind our printers."

"I guess that'll be some help," I said.

"You can also apply to the Government for financial assistance. Of course, you can't have the entire mid-Pacific declared a disaster area, but I'm sure you can get some help from a number of Government agencies."

"I see." Suddenly there was nothing left to talk about. I started to get up from my chair. "Well, thank you for your time, Dr. Rossman."

"I'm sorry to have to disappoint you."

"My father's going to be the one who's disappointed."

He walked me to the door of his office.. "Can you come back tomorrow? I can put you in touch with the people who will make the arrangements for this realtime forecasting."

I nodded. "All right. I wasn't planning to leave until tomorrow afternoon anyway."

"Good. We'll do everything we can for you."

I walked down the hallway, past the now-empty office where Ted and Dr. Barneveldt had been, and made my way back to the lobby. The building seemed completely deserted now, and I was feeling awfully alone.

Ted was slouched across one of the couches in the lobby, thumbing through a magazine. He looked up at me.

"Dr. Bee figured you might not have any transportation back to town. Tough to get a cab around this time. Need a lift?"

"Thanks. Are you going into Boston?"

"Live in Cambridge, just across the river. Come on."

His car was a battered old Lotus two-seater. He gunned it out of the parking lot and onto the beltway, engine howling, and roared down a manual-control lane. Probably the car had no electronic guidance equipment, I thought.

It had been a long time since I'd been in New England in April; I'd forgotten how chilly it can be. Zooming through the twilight, and still wearing my Island sports clothes, I could feel my teeth start to chatter. Ted was happily unaware of this. He talked steadily over the growl of the engine and the whistling cold wind, gesturing with one hand and steering through the thickening traffic with the other. His monologue changed tack almost as often as he switched driving lanes: he talked about Rossman, Dr. Barneveldt, something about turbulent air flow, mathematics, air pollution, and even threw in a quick lecture on the peculiarities of Hawaii's climate. I nodded and shivered. Every time he zipped past another car I wished we were on the automatically controlled section of the highway.

He dropped me at the hotel I told him I wanted, after raising his eyebrows in mock respect at the mention of its name. "Fanciest place in town; you travel top class."

My room was comfortable. And heated. I was surprised, though, that the hotel wouldn't give me a suite. Too many people and not enough floor space, the registration clerk told me. I ordered a wardrobe by viewphone—nothing too much, just some slacks and a jacket, and incidentals.

Dinner felt strangely like lunch until I realized that my body was still on Hawaii time. I was far from sleepy even at midnight, so I watched the all-night TV movies until I finally drifted off.

The sun rose brightly across the western half of the globe, its unfailing energy heating the seas and continents—and the restless, heaving ocean of air that mantled them both. Powered by the sun, twisted by the spinning Earth beneath it, the atmosphere moved like a living, throbbing creature. Winds and currents pulsed through it. Gigantic columns of air billowed upward for miles and sank again, absorbed moisture and released it, borrowed warmth from the tropics and carried it poleward, breathed life wherever they touched. Above this endless activity, the turbulent air ocean became more placid, except for the racing rivers of the jet streams. Higher still, electrical charges swirled through a darkening sky where meteors flashed and unbreathable gases blocked all but a small slice of the sun's mighty radiance. Pulled by lunar and solar tides, mixed with magnetic fields and ghostly interplanetary winds, the ocean of air gradually thinned away and disappeared on the dark shore of space.

I slept late, dressed hurriedly, and got a rental car for the ride out to the Climatology Division. While the auto guided itself through the impossible crush of Boston traffic, I bought the best breakfast that the tinny vending machine in the back seat had to offer: synthetic juice, a warmed-over bun, and powdered milk.

I phoned ahead as the car threaded its way to the throughway and picked up speed. Dr. Rossman's secretary answered that he was busy but would detail someone to meet me in the lobby.

Climatology's parking lot was jammed now, and the lobby fairly bustled with people. I announced myself to the receptionist, who nodded to a lovely slim blonde sitting near the desk.

She was dressed in a light-green sweater and skirt, touched off with the fresh, outdoor fragrance of flower fields.

"I'm Priscilla Barneveldt," she said. "Dr. Rossman asked me to see that you got through the Services Section without trouble."

Her eyes were grayish-green, I noticed. Her face was a

trifle on the long side, but well put together, with firm features and a determined little chin.

"Well," I said, "you're the most pleasant surprise I've had in the whole Weather Bureau so far."

"And that's the most pleasant compliment I've heard all day . . . so far." She spoke with a slight, unidentifiable accent. "The elevators are down this way."

"Don't forget your glasses, Barney," the receptionist said.

"Oh, thanks." She went back to the chair she had been sitting in and picked up the eyeglasses. "I'd be squinting all day without them."

"Barney?" I asked as we walked to the elevators.

A trace of a smile shaped her lips. "It's better than 'Prissy,' or 'Silly,' don't you think?"

"I guess so." The elevator doors slid open and we stepped inside. "But isn't it a little confusing?"

She really smiled now. "I'm afraid I'm not a very highly organized person . . . not with people, anyway. Third floor please," she said to the elevator control panel.

It took nearly an hour for me to fill out the forms in the Services Section that would send Dr. Rossman's up-to-the-minute predictions to our Honolulu offices. Barney helped me with them and fed the finished paperwork into the automatic processor that made up most of the Section.

Then she said, "Have you seen the rest of the building? I could give you the official guided tour, if you like."

Nothing could have bored me more, I thought. Except sitting in the airport, waiting for the afternoon flight. "Okay, guide me."

The tour took the remainder of the morning. The building was much larger than it appeared from the outside, and even had an annex out back where the shops and maintenance equipment were kept. Barney showed me the laboratories where men and women were studying the nature of air at various pressures and temperatures—its chemical composition, the way it absorbs heat energy, the effects of water vapor, dust particles, and thousands of other things. Then we went through the theoretical section, on our way down to the electronic computers.

"The theoreticians aren't much to see," she told me as we passed their cubbyhole office. "They sit at their desks and write equations that we have to solve down at the computations center."

The computations area was impressive. Row upon row of massive computer consoles, chugging away, tapes spinning in their spools, girls scurrying, print-out typers spewing out long folding sheets of incomprehensible numbers and symbols.

"This is where I work," Barney said over the noise of the machines. "I'm a mathematician."

I had to laugh. "For a not-very-highly-organized person, you certainly picked an odd occupation."

"I'm only disorganized with people," she said. "The computers are different. I get along fine with the big machines. They don't get impatient, don't have tempers. They're strictly logical, you can tell what they're going to do next, what they need. They're a lot easier to get along with than people."

"They sound pretty dull," I said.

"Well, *some* people are more exciting than others," she admitted.

"This place," I said, watching the girls who were attending the machines, "looks like a meteorologist's harem."

Barney nodded. "There've been lots of little romances blossoming here. I've often said we wouldn't have half so many men from the staff coming over here with requests for special programming if we had male programmers."

"Girls work cheaper, I guess."

"And better, as far as detail and accuracy are concerned," Barney said firmly.

"Sorry . . . I spoke before I thought. It's a bad habit of mine. I didn't mean to imply. . . ."

"It's all right," she said, smiling.

To change the subject, I said, "I met a Dr. Barneveldt last night. Is he your father or grandfather or. . . ."

"Uncle," Barney answered. "Jan Barneveldt. He received the Nobel Prize for his work on the physical chemistry of air. He developed the first cloud-seeding chemicals that work on non-supercooled clouds."

It sounded important, even though I hadn't the faintest idea of what she was talking about.

"My father is Hannes Barneveldt; he and my mother are at the Stromlo Observatory in South Africa."

"Astronomers."

"Father is. Mother's a mathematician. They work together."

I had to smile. "Then you're following in your mother's footsteps."

"Yes, that's right. . . . Come this way." She took my arm and guided me through the ranks of computer consoles. "There's something no guided tour would be complete without."

We stepped through a door into darkness. Barney shut the door behind us and the din of the computers was cut off. The room was cool and softly quiet. Only gradually, as my eyes adjusted to the low lighting level, did I realize what was there.

I heard myself gasp.

We were standing before a twenty-foot-high viewscreen that showed the entire western hemisphere. I could make out the North and South American continents clearly, even though clouds obscured broad stretches of land and sea. The Arctic glittered dazzlingly, and the sweep of colors— blue, green, red, white—was literally breathtaking.

On the other side of the room, the other side of the world: Europe, Africa, Asia, the broad Pacific, covered in their entirety by two more viewscreens.

"This never fails to awe people," Barney said softly. "Including me, no matter how often I see it."

"It's . . ." I groped for a word, ". . . unbelievable."

"The pictures are being transmitted from the synchronous space stations. We can see the entire world's weather patterns at a glance."

She walked to the podium that stood in the center of the room. A few touches on the control switches there, and weather maps sprang up on the viewscreens, superimposed on the televised pictures.

"We can backtrack," she said, her fingers flickering across the controls, "and see what the weather maps looked like yesterday . . ." the map shifted and changed slightly, "or the day before . . . or last week . . . last year. . . ."

"What about tomorrow, or next week, or next year?"

"Tomorrow's no problem." The map shifted again. I

could see that the storm now covering the area where Thornton dredges were trying to operate would lift off by tomorrow.

"We can give you an educated guess about next week," Barney said, "but it's so vague that we don't bother making up the maps for it. As for next year," she lowered her voice conspiratorially, "you'll have to consult the *Old Farmer's Almanac.* That's what we all do."

"Is that what Ted Marrett does?"

Surprised, she asked, "Do you know Ted?"

"We met last night. Didn't your uncle tell you?"

"No, he didn't mention it. He's rather forgetful; it's sort of a family trait."

"Is Ted here? I'd like to talk to him."

"He's at MIT in the morning," Barney said. "We generally see him at lunch."

I glanced at my wristwatch. Almost noon.

"Where do you eat?"

"There's a cafeteria here in the building. Would you like to join us?"

"If you don't mind."

"I warn you," she said seriously, "there's usually nothing but shoptalk."

"If the shoptalk's about weather control, I want to hear it."

3. Aerodynamics, Plus Water

The Climatology Division's cafeteria was large, very crowded and noisy, and terribly depressing. The walls were painted dead gray, and the few attempts someone had made at decorations had long ago faded into near-oblivion. Streams of people jostled through the lines and crowded the bare plastic tables. There was practically no real food at all, just synthetics and concentrates. Hardly appetizing, although Barney seemed to be pleased enough with the selection.

"Aren't you hungry?" she asked me as we hunted for an unoccupied table.

My tray was nearly empty. "I . . . uh, I guess I'm used to Island food," I lied clumsily.

"There are better restaurants in the towns nearby, and in Boston, of course. But they're pretty expensive."

"Real meat is worth the money," I said.

She gave me a funny look, then dropped the subject.

By the time we found a table and sat down, Ted had arrived.

"That's Tuli Noyon with Ted," Barney told me as they took trays and started working their way down the chow line. "Tuli's from Mongolia. Ted met him at MIT and got him a part-time job here. He's a chemical kineticist."

"A what?"

"Chemical kineticist," she said again. "Tuli's been working with my uncle on new chemical catalysts that can change the energy balance of an air mass."

"Oh. Something like cloud seeding?"

"Sort of."

Tuli had a stocky build that disguised his height; but I saw that he was nearly as tall as Ted. His face was oval, brown-skinned, flat featured—more like an Eskimo's than any Oriental I had ever seen before.

As the two of them weaved through the crowded tables toward us, I could see that they were deep in conversation, with Ted doing most of the talking. He was balancing a heavily loaded tray with one hand and gesticulating vividly with the other. Tuli was nodding, his round face nearly expressionless.

I rose as they put their trays down on our table. Ted nodded a greeting at Barney and me without breaking vocal stride:

"So Gustafson's agreed to let me use the MIT computer on the midnight-to-four shift, if I can get somebody to program it. That's where you come in, Barney."

Tuli, who had remained standing, said to me, "I am Tuli Noyon, a friend and associate of this red-headed talking machine."

I had to laugh. "I'm Jerry Thorn." We shook hands and sat down.

"So I forgot to introduce you," Ted muttered, already

digging into his food. "More important things percolating in my skull. Barney, you've got to squeeze some time to program the MIT machine for me. And maybe bootleg a little time on the computer here. It's for a good cause."

"It's always for a good cause." But she was smiling at him.

"Ted has almost convinced me," Tuli said, "that he can make pinpoint weather forecasts two or three weeks in advance."

"By using the turbulence equations?" Barney asked.

Ted nodded at her as he swallowed a forkful of imitation steak.

"Will your two-week forecast be better than the Weather Bureau's thirty-day predictions?" I asked.

He swallowed hard. "Better? No comparison, buddy. That monthly dream sheet Rossman puts out is just a general look at regional trends—temperature, rainfall for regions like New England or the Southwest. Runs about seventy-five percent accurate on temperature, less'n fifty percent on precipitation. Pretty punk."

"And your forecasts?"

"Ninety-five percent accuracy, plus. And pinpointed! With a little work, I'll be able to tell you which side of the street gets wet from a cloudburst. You'll be able to set your watch by these forecasts."

"That may be a slight exaggeration," Tuli said. "And although the monthly forecasts we do are very vague, the Bureau's three-day forecasts—put out by the various local centers—are generally about ninety percent accurate."

"I'm not exaggerating," Ted insisted. "And even the best forecasts the Bureau'll make only give general guesstimates on temperature, wind, and precipitation totals. Listen, I've

seen guys program old wives' tales into the computers—
you know, 'Red sky at morning, sailor take warning,' that
kind of stuff. It was just as accurate as the Bureau's daily
forecasts. Honest, I mean it! But I'm making *exact* predictions. To the degree, mile per hour of wind speed, and
tenth-inch of precipitation."

"That will be very impressive," Tuli said, "if it works."

"Okay, doubting Confucius; I did a hand calculation
for Boston for the rest of the week. If it works out okay, we
can go to the machine and do a full week for the whole
continental United States."

"Such a humble beginning," Tuli said, straight-faced.
"Why not forecast the entire summer for the whole
world?"

Ted looked at him. "Next week, maybe."

"I can see there won't be much sleep between now and
Monday," Barney said.

"Probably the rest of next week, too," Ted answered
cheerfully. "I want to do the climatological prediction for
the next three months."

Tuli said, "When you finally get your degree, you should
share it with Barney."

"I've threatened to marry her; if that doesn't scare her
off, nothing will."

Barney said nothing and the conversation seemed to stall.

"May I ask a question?"

"Sure, Jerry."

"You talked about weather forecasts and climate predictions. What's the difference?"

Ted downed the last of his protein concentrate, then
said, "What'd the Red Sox do last night?"

"Huh?"

"They won, four to nothing," he answered his own question.

"But what's that got to do with—"

He waved me down. "Night before they also won, six to five. But Monday they got clobbered, eight to one."

"A barbaric sport," Tuli murmured. "It will never replace archery."

"Each individual game," Ted went on, ignoring him, "is like a day's weather."

"You mean each one is different."

"Sure. A shutout, a slugfest, tight game, runaway . . . they're all baseball, all played under the same rules. But no two games are exactly alike. Right?"

I nodded.

"Now, where are the Sox in the standings? Fourth, isn't it? Two games behind Seattle. That's the season's climate . . . so far. Last year it was sixth place, seventeen games off the pennant winners.

"I think I see. The overall effect——"

"Of many days' weather," Ted finished for me, "makes up the climate. You can predict that the Sox will end up somewhere between third and sixth this year. That's pretty clear. But predicting the score of tomorrow's game . . . that's tough. Right?"

"I think I see."

"Okay, now if I can get you two guys to help me," he said to Barney and Tuli, "we ought to be able to pinpoint the weather for any spot in the country two or three weeks ahead. How's that for a master's thesis?"

"I don't know anything about a thesis," I said, "but it's just what I came here to talk about."

I explained, while the cafeteria slowly emptied of people,

about the storms in the Pacific and Father's dredging operations.

Ted listened quietly, then said, "It's been a bad year out there, all right. Always is during a sunspot minimum. But you need more than accurate forecasts. You need weather control."

"I asked Dr. Rossman about that, and he said it's impossible."

"That's right, it is . . . to him."

"But to you?"

He hunched closer to the table, lowering his voice in the growing quietness of the cafeteria. "Listen. What do you need for weather control? First, you need detailed info on what's going on, the real weather at the moment. We've got that. Second, you've got to be able to make changes in the weather, where and when you want 'em. Real changes, not just ripples. Guys like Tuli and Dr. Barneveldt are turning out dandy chemicals for seeding clouds and changing energy balances. And the Air Force has lasers in orbit that'll fry eggs from a thousand miles out."

He took a gulp of coffee, then resumed. "Third, you need to know the atmosphere's heat budget—energy balance— all around the world. We can do that, right now. Last, you have to be able to forecast with pinpoint accuracy what the weather all over the world will be for weeks or months ahead. Then you can see what effects your weather changes'll make. You don't dare try squashing a storm if you're afraid it'll cause a blizzard in Florida."

It sounded logical. "I see. Now, you're working on that last item, the long-range weather forecasts with pinpoint accuracy."

"By the end of next week we ought to know if we can do it. Think we can."

"And you really believe," Barney said, with a slight frown of concentration, "that the turbulence equations are the key to accurate long-range forecasts."

"They're the whole show!" Ted insisted. "Listen. Weather is nothing more than turbulent airflow . . . simple aerodynamics, plus water." He turned to me and went on, "The water's what makes it tricky . . . can be vapor, liquid or solid . . . can release heat or soak it up . . . and most of what we really want out of a weather prediction is info on when and how much rain or snow we'll get. Right?"

I nodded.

"Okay. From an aerodynamicist's viewpoint, the weather's just a boundary layer problem . . . air rubbing against the surface of the Earth. But it's a *turbulent* boundary layer, that makes it a tough problem. When you feel a wind, it's hardly ever a strong, smooth, steady flow, is it? It comes in gusts, spurts, never the same for more than a second or two. It's turbulent!"

"Turbulent flow," Tuli explained, "means that the fluid has motion in two planes—horizontally and vertically. Air is in turbulent motion throughout the troposphere, the lowest part of the atmosphere. Above the tropopause. . . ."

"That's the upper boundary of the troposphere," Barney added. "Usually about twenty to forty thousand feet altitude."

"Yes," Tuli said. "Above the tropopause is the so-called stratosphere. The airflow there is almost entirely laminar; it flows horizontally, with very little vertical motion."

My head was beginning to spin. "Wait a minute. One

of you, I forget which, said air is a fluid. Did I hear that right?"

"Fluids can be liquids, gases, or plasmas," Tuli answered.

"Get the picture?" Ted resumed. "What we call weather only happens in the troposphere . . . and it's in turbulent flow. Above the tropopause, no turbulence and no weather to speak of."

"There are jet streams up there," Tuli said. "They have considerable effect on the weather."

"Sure. And if you go farther up there're electrical effects in the ionosphere, and magnetic storms from solar flares, and cosmic particles and whatnot. But they're second- or third-order effects. Don't really make much difference in the day-to-day weather down here. Might have some long-range climatological effects, though."

"But the actual weather happens in turbulent air," I said, trying to get it straight.

"Check. And because it's turbulent, there was no real way to predict it, until these Kraichnan Institute studies showed that you can determine what's happening in a turbulent flow. What I've done is to use the Kraichnan work, apply it to weather forecasting. If it works, we'll be able to really *predict* the weather, instead of trying to outguess it."

"But how are weather forecasts made now? They seem to be pretty good, even without this turbulence business."

Ted grinned and leaned back in his chair. "How do they do it now? Lots of ways. Flipping coins, playing numbers games on the computers, waiting for twinges in toes or knees. . . ."

"Ted, be fair," Tuli said. "The principal technique is the method of persistence. . . ."

"You look at the weather around you," Ted took up, "and try to figure out what's heading your way and how fast it's moving. Gets complicated, but it works pretty well for the short term—couple days or so."

Tuli added, "We can 'see' all around the globe now, thanks to satellites. And detailed mathematical models allow the meteorologists to forecast with some accuracy how the weather patterns will move across the Earth's surface."

"Still a lot of hunchwork in it," Ted insisted.

Tuli nodded agreement.

"It's slightly bewildering," I said. Looking around, I could see that we were the last ones in the cafeteria.

"They're closing up," Barney said. "If we don't want to get the floor-scrubbers showering us. . . ."

"Okay, back to work," Ted agreed.

We got up and headed for the door.

"But you're really serious," I asked him, "about this weather-control idea?"

For the first time, Tuli let a smile break across his stolid expression. "Better ask him a harder question: like, does he intend to breathe all afternoon."

"It's that definite," I said as we went through the doorway and into the hall.

"If this forecasting scheme works," Ted answered, "there's only one thing more that we'll need."

"What's that?"

"Permission."

"Is that all? Why, Dr. Rossman should be glad to give you the go-ahead."

Ted shook his head. "It's a new idea. And what's worse, it's not *his* idea."

A mountain was being built. Vaster than the Alps, higher than the Himalayas, an immense, invisible mountain of air was forming over the Atlantic Ocean between Bermuda and the mainland of America. From high aloft, cold, dense air was sinking down, weighted by its low temperature, and piling up at the ocean's surface. The mountain grew and spread, real as a peak of rock. But this mountain moved. It swirled in clockwise rotation, pivoting over the ocean, winds flowing out from its edges across land and sea. The high-pressure system pushed its western frontier nearly a hundred miles inland of the American coast. Warm, semitropical air from the Caribbean and Gulf of Mexico was pulled northward by the clockwise flow, streamed across the East Coast, bringing warmth and moisture with it. Some of the warm air, lighter and more buoyant than the high-pressure mountain, rode up over the colder, denser air mass. As it rose it cooled; the water vapor in it condensed and fell as showers. Meteorologists talked about the Bermuda High. But the people in Boston's streets simply said, "Spring is here. It's come at last."

I drove back to my hotel room through the gentle spring shower, my stomach rumbling from lack of lunch, and my mind racing to figure out what I would say to Father. I phoned Thornton Aerospace from the car and canceled my reservation back to Hawaii. At the hotel, I told the desk that I would be staying indefinitely and then ordered lunch. Finally, I called Father.

"And that's what Dr. Rossman said," I told him, after a fifteen-minute explanation of the situation. "He can give us extended forecasts, but controlling the storms is impossible, as far as he's concerned."

Father scowled. "That's not going to be enough to help us, Jeremy."

"I know."

The videophone was sitting on the coffee table, next to my lunch tray. I got up from the sofa and paced across the room.

"Stop fidgeting and stay where I can see you!" Father snapped.

I sat on the windowsill, beside the softly humming air blower, and glanced at the thronged streets far below.

"So all we can do is sit here and hope the Climatology Division can warn us of the storms in time to keep us from losing people?" Father's face wore the expression he uses when he thinks about how much he pays in taxes and how little he gets back in return.

"There's another side to it, Dad. Some of the people at Climatology think weather control can be done. But not right away."

I told him about Ted's hopes.

"How serious is this fellow?" Father demanded. "Is he a pipe dreamer or can we depend on him?"

"I think he's dependable. This Dr. Barneveldt—he won the Nobel Prize, you know—he seems to be working with Ted pretty closely. So it can't be completely haywire."

"Scientists can be wrong, Jeremy. Even Nobel Prize winners."

"Well, maybe. But I think I'd like to stay here a while and see what happens. Ted might have the answer we want. Even his long-range predictions by themselves could be very important for us."

Father nodded. "I agree, although I'm not certain you're the one who should be keeping track of him. You're a long way from home, young man."

"I can take care of myself. And the family's just a few minutes' drive from here."

"Have you seen your uncles or Aunt Louise yet?"

"Not yet. But I'll drop in on them."

"Yes, I suppose you couldn't very well stay in Boston without visiting them," Father said reluctantly. "Give them my regards. And don't overplay this storm problem."

"Yes, sir."

"And stay as close as you can to this Marrett fellow. He may be a crackpot, but he's the only hope we have."

Staying close to Ted was no easy task. Mornings he was at MIT, afternoons at the Climatology offices, and evenings he was apt to be working either at one place or the other. He was a man on the move.

Barney tipped me off that he usually spent an hour or so Saturday mornings at the Cambridge YMCA, not far from the apartment he shared with Tuli.

I cornered him there, in a small gym off the main basketball court, and watched him give a fencing lesson to Tuli. Standing still, in the heavy white jacket and fencing mask, he looked like a hulking, heavy-footed gladiator. I expected Tuli to outspeed him easily. But in action he moved with the lightning grace of a leopard.

"Played halfback in college," he explained at the end of the session, his face soaked with sweat. "Where I got my nose conked. Had a captain in the Air Force who liked fencing. He taught me and I'm teaching Tuli. Tried to get Barney interested, too, but she gave it up after a few weeks. Great stuff, you ought to try it."

We started out of the gym as Tuli said, "On alternate Saturdays we practice karate. Then I'm the teacher and he's the student."

"Not enough action in karate," Ted said, slinging his fencing bag over one shoulder. "Spend all your time in exercises and Oriental meditation."

As we headed for the locker room, Ted suddenly suggested, "How about a quick swim? We've got about twenty minutes to spare. Come on, Jerry, we'll dig up a suit for you."

I agreed quickly. We raced two laps and I outdistanced him easily. "Doggone fish," he called out, treading water. "Forgot you're an Islander. Come on, let's try it again."

It was a challenge to him. A test he couldn't ignore. After half a dozen laps he was keeping up with me. He didn't have the right coordination, but he thrashed along on brute force, just about matching me, stroke for stroke.

"Looks as though you can do everything," I said as we finally hauled ourselves out of the pool.

"No sense trying to do anything unless you can do it right," he answered.

While we dressed in the locker room, Tuli said quietly to me, "He's the type who either excels in what he's doing, or simply doesn't do it. He's about as good in karate now as I am, although I've been studying the art for years and he's been at it only a few months."

"He's an unusual person," I agreed.

"When I first came to MIT last year," Tuli added, "Ted was the only one to accept me right away. My English was terrible, of course. He shared his apartment with me and spent two solid months working on my pronunciation. There are not many like him."

After we were dressed, Ted suggested we get an early lunch.

"Here at the Y?" I asked.

He nodded.

"I've got to see some people in Boston," I lied.

Shrugging, he said, "Okay. See you soon."

He turned for the locker-room door.

"I wanted to ask you," I said, walking alongside him, "how the long-range forecasts are going."

That brought a smile. "Great, so far. The hand calculation I did the middle of the week looks solid. This morning's official forecast by the Boston Weather Bureau office is just the same as mine . . . but not as detailed, of course."

"And yours was made three days ago."

"Four. We've got the MIT computer running off the detailed forecast for the coming week. Should be finishing the run tonight. Then it's just the dogwork of checking everything out . . . got the whole country to check on for the next eight days, Sunday to Sunday."

"And you have half the MIT Department of Meteorology and three-fourths of Climatology's computer section helping you," Tuli said, pushing the locker-room door open.

"That many? Good . . . we'll need 'em. And more."

I asked, "Does Dr. Rossman know about all this?"

Ted winced. "Hope not. At least, not yet. If he finds out how much time and manpower we're throwing into this bootlegged work. . . ."

"He might consider some Eastern methods we have of dealing with undesirables," Tuli said, straight-faced.

"By Friday we'll have the predictions for the whole country checked out for most of the week. I'll tell Rossman about it then . . . if everything's working okay."

"Why don't we celebrate?" I suggested. "We could go down to Thornton for the weekend."

"Thornton?"

"My family's place in Marblehead."

Ted glanced at Tuli. "Okay, why not? Maybe a celebration'll be in order next weekend."

We shook hands on it, and I told them I'd ask Barney along, too.

"I'll ask Barney," Ted said. There was nothing really hostile in his voice when he said it, but his tone was awfully firm.

4. Barney

~~~~~~~~~~~~~~~

IT WAS Sunday afternoon before I heard from any of them again. I was in my hotel room, watching TV, when the phone rang. To my surprise, it was Barney.

"Ted just told me that you've invited us to Marblehead for next weekend."

"That's right." I nodded. "I hope you can come."

"I don't see why not. And it's very sweet of you to ask us. I just thought I'd warn you, though. I stole a look at Ted's forecast for the area, and it looks as though it will rain right through the weekend."

Just what we need, I said to myself. Aloud, I told her, "That's too bad; I had hoped to take you out boating. Maybe Ted's forecast won't turn out."

"Don't say that . . . he'd be heartbroken."

"I suppose so."

Shaking her head, she said, "I'd love to go sailing, though. It's a shame . . . the weather's going to be fine all week. Until late Friday."

I glanced toward the window. The Charles River was

dotted with sails. "Maybe we could go during the week . . . just a short jaunt. . . ."

"You mean after work? Would there be enough time?"

"Sure," I said.

"All right," she said happily. "How about Tuesday?"

"I'll pick you up at the Climatology building."

"Wonderful."

So that Tuesday, after a fast drive out to the suburbs and back to Boston, we went out on the Charles in a rented sailboat. We skimmed along the river, crowded with other boats and an occasional powered cruiser zigzagging noisily through the flotilla. The sun was just starting to dip down behind the Back Bay complex of towers; we could see its flaming reflection in the windows of the MIT buildings on the Cambridge side of the river.

"I'm really glad you were free tonight," I said.

"So am I," she answered, raising her voice slightly against the wind that slapped the sails. She was wearing slacks and an oversized sweater that we had found in the boat's gear chest. "Ted's kept us all terribly busy with forecasts. But I think the computer can do the rest of the work without me."

I leaned back, one hand on the tiller, and let the breeze carry us along. Barney seemed to be enjoying herself.

"Is Ted always like this?"

"Like what?" she asked.

"Well . . . sort of like an active volcano."

Barney laughed. "He's very excited about this forecasting technique. This is an important week for him."

I had to tack for mid-river as we approached the Harvard Bridge. "You two spend a lot of time together, don't you?"

"I suppose we do, between the office and this extra-curricular work of his. We've even had dates together, now and then, when he's hardly mentioned meteorology at all."

"That doesn't sound likely."

"I know," she replied, laughing again. "But it's true. At first I thought Ted was only interested in getting some extra help for his computations. He's not much of a mathematician, really. Perhaps it was only that . . . at first."

"And now?"

"Now?" She brushed a bit of spray from her cheek. "You heard him last week . . . he said he's threatened to marry me."

"And you've agreed?"

"I haven't really been asked, Jerry. I think Ted just assumes that I'm his girl and he'll marry me some day— after he's proven that he can control the weather."

"You mean he just takes you for granted like that?"

Nodding, she said, "You've got to understand him, Jerry. He's so wrapped up in his work that people . . . well, it's not that they're really secondary to him, but Ted simply doesn't worry about people unless they force him to pay attention.

"And he can't possibly do what he wants to do all by himself. He needs people to help him. So I help, and try not to cause him problems."

"That makes it convenient for him."

"I hope so. I've never met anyone like Ted. He sees farther than anyone I know, dreams bigger dreams. I suppose I'm part of his plan for the future." She hesitated. "I imagine I'm *almost* as important to him as controlling the weather."

"You deserve a better fate than that," I said.

"That's what I keep telling him."

I headed the boat back to the dock, and then we drove to one of the better student restaurants in Harvard Square and had dinner. She began asking me about Hawaii and my family. By the time dinner was finished, she was telling me about the civil war in South Africa, and how her father had saved the 150-inch telescope there from being wrecked by a renegade mob.

We took in the three-D show at the new Hologram Theater, and then drove back along the Charles to "Faculty Row," where her apartment was. She lived with her uncle, who was a visiting professor at MIT as well as a member of the Climatology staff.

"This was a lot of fun, Jerry," she said as I helped her out of the car. "I enjoyed myself immensely."

"I'm glad. We'll have to try it again, soon."

"Fine."

I wanted to kiss her, but before I could make up my mind actually to do it, she turned and walked up the steps to the apartment door. I stood there, feeling stupid, as she waved goodnight to me.

Even during those bright days of late April, the air of the Arctic was heavy with cold. It sat atop the spinning Earth, imprisoned by a constant wall of westerly winds encompassing the Arctic Circle. But as the heartlands of Asia and North America warmed under the springtime sun, complicated readjustments began to take place in the moving, dynamic atmosphere. The westerlies faltered at one spot, briefly. It was long enough for a great mass of polar air to slide out of its Arctic prison and begin flowing southward. A long chain of events followed, a chain that stretched halfway across the world. The polar air mass pushed a weaker bubble of high pressure down across the great open stretches of northern Canada. Across the length of the continent the changes and counterchanges took place, as huge masses of air jostled each other, seeking a balance, a new equilibrium. The Bermuda High began to break up under the competing pressures of other systems. A tiny low-pressure cell, no more than a few clouds off the coast of Vera Cruz, felt itself being drawn into the trough of low pressure sandwiched between two westward-flowing Highs. The little storm headed northeastward, drawing moisture and power from the sea as it traveled.

I spent the next morning at the Boston Public Library, gathering book spools on meteorology (most of which I couldn't understand, as it turned out) and arguing the chief librarian into letting me borrow them even though I wasn't a permanent resident.

I went back to my hotel room, the spools under my arm. The phone was buzzing as I unlocked the door. I called out "Hello!" to make it open the circuit, thinking it might be Barney, but when I got into the room I saw Father's face on the screen.

"So there you are," he said as I stepped before the viewscreen.

I dropped the microfilm spools on the sofa.

"Jeremy, we just got the first of the fast predictions from the Weather Bureau, together with an analysis of the coming month's weather trends."

"How does it look?"

Father shook his head. "Not good at all. I'm going to shut down all the dredging operations for the rest of the month. Three days' advance warning of a storm—which may or may not hit us—just isn't enough to work with. I'd rather close down and lose money than have the dredges wrecked or somebody killed."

"I'm sorry. . . ."

"It's not your fault. You've done the best you could. The trouble is, if we default on this contract with Modern Metals, the word will go 'round that deep-sea mining isn't reliable. That's what can really kill us."

I sat on the edge of the sofa. "Father, how would you like to have pinpoint predictions, a week or more in advance. Fully accurate."

He grunted.

"That's what Ted is working on. By the end of the month, he might be able to run off a set of predictions for us that will forecast the weather for the entire area where the dredges are working. The predictions will go two or three weeks into the future."

Father rubbed his chin thoughtfully. "If he can do that, we could keep the dredges going . . . just shut them down temporarily in advance of storm weather and then reopen them afterward. But we'd need a week's warning to make the system work."

"Ted can do it, I'm sure he can. Two weeks, at least. Then you'd know exactly when to shut the dredges down, how long they'd have to stay shut, and when you could open them again. You could schedule the storms' effects right into the operation."

"Can he really do it . . . this Marrett fellow?"

"We'll know for certain by the end of this week."

Father mulled it over for a few moments. "All right, Jeremy. I'll keep the dredges open until the end of the week. Just pray that we don't get caught with another bad storm in the meantime, that's all."

"I'll keep my fingers crossed."

Without realizing it, I had committed Ted to a very stiff assignment—without his slightest knowledge. I tried to call him, but he couldn't be reached. So I got through to Barney, in the computations section.

"I don't know when you'll be able to see Ted," she answered me. He's going to be busy tonight checking his forecasts. . . . I'll be helping him. Why don't you join us there?"

"Where?"

"At Ted's place. We're going there right after work. We'll eat there. You're welcome to join us."

"Okay, fine." Then I remembered what Ted considered food. "Um, maybe I'll meet you after dinner."

She smiled as though she could read my mind. "I'll be the cook tonight, so you might be doing the smartest thing."

"No, I didn't mean . . . that is. . . ."

"It's all right, Jerry. Don't apologize. I wouldn't want to eat soyburgers either when I could have a real steak."

"I guess I'm just a foolish snob." Then I got an idea. "Say, why don't I bring the dinner? I could have them cook up something here at the hotel and pack it in plastic dishes. You won't even have to clean up afterward!"

She looked doubtful. "That might be a little too fancy for Ted. . . ."

"I'll make it simple. And it'll save you time and trouble. Okay?"

"All right, you talked me out of working. Thanks."

I got to Ted's apartment, following Barney's directions,

just about five o'clock. The back seat of my rental car was filled with cartons. I buzzed Ted's number at the lobby phone and asked him to come down and help with the packages.

He was downstairs in half a minute, peering into the packages on the seat.

"CARE comes to Cambridge," he muttered.

We carried the cartons upstairs and had dinner. The food was excellent; even Ted seemed pleased.

"I'm beginning to see it pays to have rich friends," he said, sprawling on the little room's only sofa. "Better be careful or you'll soften me up, Jerry."

"I thought it would be easier on Barney this way."

"Get more useful work out of her, reduce entropy. Guess I can't complain about that."

Within a few minutes after finishing the meal, the one-room apartment was converted into a meteorology workshop. The only table, the sofa bed, even the sink and range in the kitchenette were covered with papers: maps, graphs, calculations, scribblings, stacks of computer print-outs. Ted and Tuli soon lapsed into a cryptic shorthand dialogue, while Barney fed them sheets of paper to read.

"Indianapolis," Ted called out.

"Seventy-three, fifty-one, ten-sixteen, point-oh-four, west twelve to eighteen," Tuli answered in singsong chant.

"Check. Memphis."

Barney stole over to my chair and whispered, "They're checking the five o'clock weather reports from selected stations around the country against the forecasts Ted made last week. So far, everything is checking to within a few percent."

"Good."

It was well past midnight when Ted finally turned over the last sheet of computer print-out and said triumphantly, "On the line, every last one of 'em. We got it, kids. We've got it cold!"

"Do you think Dr. Rossman will believe it?" Barney asked from the range. She was boiling water for instant coffee.

"He's got to," Ted snapped. "The numbers are all here and they check. He's got to buy it."

"Could you do the same thing," I asked, "for a region in the mid-Pacific?"

He turned to me. "For Thornton's dredging operations? Sure, why not? Won't be as accurate, 'cause there aren't as many observation stations out there . . . but we can make it good enough to tell your people when to button up for storms."

"How far in advance?"

He shrugged. "Week or ten days, at least. Probably two weeks."

"Great!"

"Take a lot of work," he said. "We can't go on boot-legging forever."

"Thornton can pay for it," I said.

"The first item of business," Tuli pointed out, "is to match the rest of the forecasts against the actual weather reports for the rest of the week. . . ."

"And then lay 'em under Rossman's long nose," Ted cracked, "and watch him turn green with surprise. Friday's the big day. I'll show everything to Rossman then."

"Is it still supposed to rain over the weekend?" I asked.

He nodded. "Supposed to."

"We won't be able to go sailing," I said.

"Don't give up hope. The situation could change."

I didn't realize what he meant. "You're going to come anyway, aren't you?"

"Try and stop us!"

Thursday dragged by. I read a good bit of the time, but it was tough going. Most of the books were too full of equations for me to follow; the others were written for simpletons. None of them conveyed the excitement that Ted did about the living, breathing nature of the weather. By Friday I had given up on reading and spent the day staring at the TV screen.

Sure enough, as I started to drive out to the Climatology building it began drizzling. I never saw a more dispirited trio as they walked across the parking lot in the rain and climbed into my car.

"Don't be so glum," I said. "Even if we can't sail, we can have a lot of fun at Thornton."

"It's not that," Barney said, sitting beside me.

"What's wrong?" I saw that she was on the verge of tears. In the back seat, Ted slouched back disgustedly, his chin on his chest. Even the normally impassive Tuli looked crushed.

Barney said, "Ted showed his forecasts to Dr. Rossman this afternoon."

"And?"

"He thinks they're very interesting, thank you," Ted growled, "but there's no use getting excited over what was probably a lucky accident."

"Accident?"

"That's the word he used."

"But . . . what's it mean?"

"Nothing. That's exactly what it means. We show him how to make pinpoint predictions a week in advance, and he wants to stick the idea in a drawer and forget about it!"

5. A Weather Change

"THAT'S not exactly true," Tuli said as I gunned the car's engine and started off the Climatology parking lot. "Dr. Rossman said he wants to study the new technique before he proposes it to Washington as a standard Weather Bureau forecasting method."

"Study it," Ted grumbled. "You know what that means —couple of years, at least."

"He's a cautious man," Tuli said.

"Yeah, especially with other people's ideas. He could use the system on an experimental basis and see if it works. In three months he'd have enough data to satisfy Congress, the Supreme Court, and the College of Cardinals. But not him. He's going to sit on it and play around with it until it gets to be known as *his* idea."

"You mean you won't be able to make any more long-range forecasts?" I asked.

"Not now. The idea belongs to the Climatology Division now. . . . Rossman thinks it's his private property. He told me to get back to doing the work I'm paid to do and stop trying to run the Division."

I began to feel just as dreary as the clouds above us. "What about weather control?"

"You should've seen his face when I brought that up. Told him the whole idea of these long-range forecasts is to make weather control workable. He nearly fainted. Absolutely forbade me to even mention the subject again."

We drove out to the North Shore in dismal silence. By the time we reached the causeway that connected Marblehead Neck to the mainland it was raining steadily.

"Right on the button," Ted mumbled gloomily as he stared out the car window. "Rain tonight, tomorrow, and Sunday. *They* think."

"What do you mean by that?" Barney asked.

All he would answer was, "You'll see."

The house hadn't changed much since the few summers before when I had last seen it. Thornton was big without being pretentious—a clean-lined white Colonial mansion with black shutters and a red door, a modest lawn, flowering shrubs around the front porch, and a garage, boathouse, and pier out back.

I pulled up in front of the main door, under the weather roof. Ted got out first:

"Who built this, Miles Standish?"

"No," I said, sliding out from behind the controls. "Actually, it was built well after the Revolution, and then rebuilt about a hundred years ago, after a hurricane knocked down the original house."

Ted looked at me as though he thought I might have been kidding him.

"It's beautiful," Barney said, as I helped her out of the car.

The front door opened and Aunt Louise came out toward me, arms extended. She was followed by a trio of servants.

"Jeremy, it's so *good* to see you!" She threw her arms around my neck. There was nothing I could do but stand there and take it. After a few gushy moments, I disentangled myself and introduced Barney, Tuli, and Ted.

"Welcome to Thornton," she said. "The servants will take your bags and show you to your rooms. We're planning to have dinner in an hour."

While they followed the servants upstairs, Aunt Louise practically towed me into the library.

"Now tell me truthfully," she said as the massive doors slid themselves shut behind her. "How is your father?"

"He's fine. Really. Perfect health, cantankerous disposition, full of energy. He drives my brothers and me ragged."

She smiled, but sadly. "You know he hasn't been here since your grandfather's funeral."

"And none of you have been to Hawaii since my mother died," I said. "It seems to take a funeral to get the family together."

I walked along the ceiling-high bookshelves, back to the ornate wooden desk where Grandfather Thorn used to spend rainy afternoons during my New England visits telling me how he talked *his* father into investing money on commercial airlines, after generations of Thorn shipbuilding success.

Aunt Louise followed me across the room. "Jeremy, you know your father always was a rebel. He could have run your grandfather's interests and lived right here at Thornton. He could have been head of the family, he's the oldest. But he got mixed up in that drilling thing. . . ."

"The Mohole."

"Yes, and he had an argument with your grandfather. So he ran off to Hawaii."

"And now he lives there and runs his own interests."

"But we never see each other," she said. "It isn't right."

"Well, why don't you invite him here? I think he'd be more than glad to come, if he thought you really wanted him to."

"Do you really believe he would?"

I nodded.

"I'll talk it over with your uncles tonight."

"They're both here?"

"Yes, for the weekend. They were planning a fishing trip, but it looks as if the rain will ruin everything."

For some reason I said, "Don't be too sure."

Both my uncles were completely unlike Father—and each other. Uncle Lowell was heavy-set, paunchy, balding, and loud. He liked cigars and conversation, especially when he was doing the talking. Uncle Turner was very tall and thin, rather quiet; he looked like the popular conception of a New England Yankee.

Uncle Lowell dominated the first three courses of dinner, in the chandeliered old dining room, with a monologue on how Thornton Aerospace was prospering, how the rocket transport business was definitely in the black and repaying all his risks and investment, and he was now able to devote some of his precious time and engineers to helping Uncle Turner develop the new oceangoing air-cushion ships for Thornton Shipping Lines.

Then he made a slip. Uncle Lowell mentioned that one problem of the air-skimming ships would be avoiding storms at sea, since they couldn't operate over storm waves.

Ted stepped in quickly, fork in hand, and took over the conversation. From storms at sea, he moved to long-range weather forecasts and weather control. Through the entree, salad, and dessert Ted held all of us—even the reluctant Uncle Lowell—fascinated.

"What I could never understand," Aunt Louise said, "is why the weather here in New England is so changeable."

"It's not just New England," Ted said, leaning back in his chair now that dessert was finished. "The whole region between the Horse Latitudes and the Polar Easterlies has the same problem. We're in the region of westerly airflow— the Temperate Zone: meaning winter blizzards, spring floods, summer droughts, and autumn hurricanes."

That brought a laugh.

"See, in this westerly flow you've got storms and fair-weather Highs chasing each other like horses on a merry-go-round." He twirled a finger through the air. "One right after the other. Never the same weather for more'n a few days—sometimes a few hours. New England is close enough to the sea to get lots of moisture, and far enough north to get practically pure polar air. Mix 'em together and you've got a king-sized blizzard. But farther away from the ocean the temperature extremes are a lot worse. Ocean's a heat sink—soaks up heat in summer to keep you cool, and gives off heat in winter to warm you."

"What about this drought problem?" Uncle Turner asked quietly. "I understand the spring rains haven't been up to normal."

Ted nodded. "And the runoff's been punk too; not enough snow last winter. We're sliding into a low-precipitation situation. We're studying it pretty closely. Don't want a water shortage if we can help it."

"Could this weather control you mentioned prevent a drought?" Uncle Turner asked.

Ted shrugged elaborately. "Sure . . . once it gets a chance to work."

"The idea of weather control gives me the chills," Uncle Lowell said. "No offense to present company, but I don't like to think of some bright young engineers tinkering with *my* weather. Too much could go wrong."

"That's the kind of spirit that kept Columbus in port twenty years," Ted flashed. "Talk like that nearly kept this country off the moon."

"Now hold on, I was never against the moon project; always knew it would pay off handsomely. But fooling around with the weather. . . ."

"Man already changes the weather, every blasted day. Smokestacks make weather, if you put enough of 'em together. Ever fly over a city at sunrise? Watch the factories starting up, you'll see man-made weather, all right. Every time a builder rips up another acre of grass and paves it over we change the weather."

"But I mean——"

"And in Israel they've even changed the climate by planting trees and irrigating 'em. Turned a desert into a forest inside of a generation. The Russians've used trees for windbreaks to force moist winds from Lake Baikal up to an altitude where they reach condensation temperature and drop rain."

Tuli nodded at that.

"But that's a lot different from trying to control the

weather altogether," Uncle Lowell protested. "You can't have scientists running around the country doing anything that pops into their heads. . . . That could be dangerous."

"Be a lot more dangerous," Ted countered, "if you didn't have people trying to do what they think's possible. You can't sit on ideas—the world'll come to a stop. People moan about technology moving too fast and ruining all the true beauty of the world. And at the same time they're hopping jets for weekends in Spain and lining up for cancer vaccine. Let 'em moan! I'll work on tomorrow, they can dream about yesterday all they want. Yesterday is finished and we can't make it better. But we can build tomorrow. Why shouldn't we control the weather? Why should we sit inside and just let it rain? Think we should've stayed away from fire and lived in caves all this time?"

Uncle Lowell, for once, was speechless.

Aunt Louise turned to Barney and said loudly enough to fill the sudden silence, "Would you like to see the rest of the house while the gentlemen finish their discussion?"

As they left, Uncle Lowell took a cigar from his jacket and lit it. "I don't know if I agree with you or not," he said to Ted, between puffs of thick blue smoke. "But stick to your guns, kid. You believe in what you say, and that's half the battle. More than half."

That night, strange changes took place in the atmosphere over New England. The edge of a high-pressure system that had been sitting over northern Maine abruptly started to weaken. Pressure began falling in a small area out to sea. The storm that had been soaking the Boston area suddenly felt the "downhill" pull of falling pressure to the north and east, and started moving off toward Nova Scotia.

I was awakened by the glare of sunlight streaming through my bedroom windows. Groggily, I sat up and looked outside. The clouds were breaking up! Sunlight was glinting on the ocean.

"Phone," I commanded, "get the weather forecast."

The phone clicked to itself for a few moments, then the speaker came on with the Weather Bureau's tape:

". . . winds northeasterly, fifteen to twenty miles per hour. Today, rain, occasionally moderate to heavy. Tonight, rain continuing. Sunday, rain ending in the late afternoon, winds shifting to westerly. Sunday night, scattered clouds, westerly winds. . . ."

There were scattered clouds outside right now, and the wind was coming from the west, I was willing to bet. I pulled on a robe, stuffed my feet into some slippers I found in the closet, and rushed downstairs. Ted was in the kitchen, at the breakfast bar, surrounded by bacon, eggs, pancakes, milk, butter, syrup, toast and jelly.

He looked up from a heavily laden fork. "Good morning."

"It certainly is," I said. "Much better than the Weather Bureau is forecasting."

Ted grinned but said nothing.

"Did you have a hand in this? Did you really. . . ."

He silenced me with a gesture. "You wanted to go sailing today, didn't you? We can talk then."

The cook was at the far end of the room, and from beyond the dining-room door I could hear Uncle Lowell's voice. He loved to read the morning news aloud to anyone within earshot.

It took a little time for the four of us to get organized

that morning, but finally we were on the ketch *Arlington*, threading through the forest of masts in crowded old Marblehead harbor, heading for the open sea.

Ted and Tuli were forward, handling the sails for me. I was at the wheel, giving orders, with Barney sitting beside me.

"You look very nautical," I said. She was wearing white slacks and a red-and-blue sailor top.

"Thank you. I forgot to pack sports clothes, so your aunt gave me this outfit. It's a throwaway, made of paper fiber. Like they wear at Moonbase."

"Seems a shame to throw away anything that looks so pretty."

"But you can't wash it."

"Well, there are plenty more copies of it," I said, "and, anyway, it wouldn't look half as pretty on anyone else."

"Flattery."

"Truth."

We reached the deep swells of the open ocean, under a sparkling sky dotted by a few tattered remains of grayish clouds. A strong west wind filled the ketch's sails, and the four of us gathered in the cockpit to relax. It was cold enough for sweatshirts and coffee.

"So this weather is made to order," I said to Ted.

"Sort of," he replied. "Storm would've lifted off tomorrow, late in the afternoon. We just modified things a little to speed up the change."

"But how did you do it?"

"Wasn't too tough. Got some buddies of mine in an Air Force satellite to squirt their lasers at the right place . . . added a little heat to the High that was holding the storm over Boston. And one of the Climatology planes was making a practice run for Dr. Barneveldt, dropping cloud-seeding pellets. I just told them where to do the dumping, and when. That set up some low pressure for the storm to slide into. So it moved away. Ought to be going up the Bay of Fundy by now."

Barney looked worried. "Aren't you afraid of getting the people who helped you into trouble? You had no authorization. . . ."

"They didn't do anything more than they would've normally done," Ted replied, a trifle impatiently. "The Air Force guys in the satellites have to run their lasers a certain number of times every day, to make sure they're combat-ready. It's part of their regular routine. Did it myself a gillion times when I was wearing a blue suit. And the Climatology plane was going to make a night run for your uncle. So they flew to one spot over the ocean instead of another. So who cares?"

Tuli said, "I hope Dr. Rossman is as nonchalant about this as you are. He generally doesn't like to have his employees doing things without his knowledge . . . and written approval."

"Listen," Ted snapped. "He claimed weather control is impossible. Now I can show him it's not. It's that simple."

Which turned out to be the understatement of the year.

6. Frontal Squall

∧∧∧∧∧∧∧∧∧∧∧∧∧∧∧

THE rest of the weekend was pleasant but inconsequential. Aunt Louise threw one of her usual Saturday-night parties, and invited half the island, including a couple of Japanese families—presumably for Tuli's benefit. I met a lot of people I hadn't seen since my last summer at Thornton, several years earlier. Aunt Louise kept steering me toward every girl in the house who was unmarried and over fifteen, while Ted stuck with Barney. Inevitably, someone brought out a guitar and folk singing started. Unexpectedly, though, Tuli turned out to be the hit of the evening when he began singing old Mongol sagas and translating them for us; most of them were fiercely violent, but some were poetic and haunting.

Before we left on Monday morning, Aunt Louise promised to invite Father to Thornton for my birthday celebration. My real birthday wouldn't be for another several months, but she intended to have a party for me within the next few weeks, since we weren't sure how long I would stay in Boston.

I drove the three of them to the Climatology building. Ted and Tuli hopped from my car to the weather-beaten Lotus, which Ted had left in the parking lot for the weekend, and took off for the morning's classes at MIT.

Barney, sitting beside me, waved as Ted cut in front of us and zoomed out toward the highway.

"How do you think Dr. Rossman's going to react to Ted's weather modification?" I asked her.

She let her worry show on her face. "He'll probably find out about it this morning, before Ted comes back from class."

"Do you think there might be serious trouble?"

"Dr. Rossman can be very strict about people doing things without his permission," Barney said. "And Ted has a short temper, too."

We sat in silence for a few minutes. It was still a little early for the main shift; a few cars were starting to pull up and park. Off on the horizon, toward the west, I could see dark clouds starting to gather.

"Perhaps I should try to stick around and talk with Ted after lunch," I said.

She thought it over before replying. "It might be a good idea if you offer to speak to Dr. Rossman, together with Ted. With a third party in the room, they might both be calmer and quieter."

"Like a referee?"

She nodded.

I thought to myself that the innocent bystander in the middle usually gets hit from both sides. Then I saw how terribly serious Barney was, how really worried she looked.

"All right, I'm game to try it."

"But you won't tell Ted you're trying to referee his argument with Dr. Rossman, will you?"

"Oh? Then how do I get to go in with him?"

"Let me handle it," she said.

I agreed with a shrug. We walked into the building, while the storm clouds advanced and darkened.

The warm air mass over New England was being invaded by a strong, cold flow sweeping out of Canada. The invasion was marked by a battlefront. The front line, hundreds of miles long, was a thick tangle of black clouds that flashed lightning and boomed thunder, spreading rain and hail over the ground below. Like most battlefronts, this one smelled of violence. Towering thunderhead clouds reared eight miles high, black and terrible, each one a complex engine of turbulent fury. The thunderheads were a savage no-man's-land of hundred-knot updrafts and downdrafts racing furiously side by side, where an unwary plane could be snapped like a twig. The invading clouds rolled onward, battering the ground with hailstones and blinding rain, racking the air with lightning, even boiling up into the stratosphere where the strong smooth winds flattened the cloud tops into anvil heads. Pressing onward, the cold invading airflow forced the yielding warm mass to surrender its moisture, to contribute its heat energy to the violent frontal line of squalls. But as the warm air retreated before the ruthless invader, its vapor-borne heat softened the cold airflow, warmed it, until the frontal squalls broke up and disappeared, leaving only a few isolated thunderheads to grumble uncertainly before they too were dissipated beneath the constant sun.

I watched the squall develop from the window of Ted's office, where Barney left me to spend the morning. I saw the wind come up, and the outside lights turn on as the skies thickened; saw the first drops splatter and then sheets of rain sweep the parking lot below me, hailstones bouncing off the car roofs. For all its violence, though, the storm passed quickly. The sun came out and started drying the puddles. I turned and saw by the clock on the wall that less than an hour had passed.

Ted shared the office with Tuli. It was a tiny room, the same size as Dr. Barneveldt's cell. Jammed into it were two desks, a pair of filing cabinets, two bookcases bolted one on top of the other, and three electric coffeepots sitting in a row on the windowsill. Ted drank coffee the way bears go for honey, and he hated waiting for a fresh pot to perk, Barney explained. So he kept three pots going constantly.

On top of each desk was a fax copy of the morning weather report for the entire northern hemisphere. I leafed through it, and saw that there was another storm building up in the Pacific.

Then I remembered: Father!

I put through a long-distance call, charging it to my hotel number. When Father's face appeared on the screen he was bleary and unshaven.

"It is four in the morning here, Jeremy," he said in a slow, barely controlled growl. "Since Friday afternoon I have tried to reach you six times, to no avail. The dredges are still operating, but I have not heard from you about this long-range prediction system. Your story had better be good."

"I'm sorry I got you out of bed, Dad. . . . I forgot about the time difference. And, uh, my news isn't really very good, either, I'm afraid."

I explained about Dr. Rossman's refusal to put Ted's

scheme into immediate operation, and Ted's deliberate tampering with the weather. Strangely, Father smiled, as I told him about it.

"The boy's got guts," he said.

Father always admired people who stood up to their superiors—as long as he wasn't the superior being stood up to.

"Yes," I said, "but what are you going to do about the dredges? There's another storm building up in the area. . . ."

"I didn't know that. I haven't seen the morning forecasts yet. It's very rare that I'm up this early."

I winced.

"I suppose, Jeremy, there's nothing we can do except shut down the dredges for the rest of the spring season. Or until your friend Marrett gets a go-ahead for his long-range forecasts. I'll try to get an extension on our contract with Modern Metals, but we're going to get a black eye on this one, boy."

Ted was crackling with nervous energy at lunch, like a fighter trained to a fine edge before facing the champion.

"Jerry volunteered to see Dr. Rossman," Barney said as we sat down in the cafeteria. "He can give a personal account of the effect on the weather that you caused."

Ted nodded eagerly. "Good idea. An unprejudiced witness."

Barney hunched forward over the table so we could hear her over the clattering din. "I don't know if it would be better for him to see Dr. Rossman before you do, or to go in with you."

"We can go in together," Ted decided, "all four of us. Overpower the old boy."

I looked at Barney. She was smiling.

Dr. Barneveldt came up to our table and put a hand on Ted's shoulder. "I understand you did some experimenting Friday night."

Ted grinned. "A little. Those new pellets of yours worked pretty well."

"Do you have the data from the monitoring planes? I'd like to see it."

Tuli said, "There were no monitoring planes. Only the plane carrying the seeding materials."

Dr. Barneveldt's face fell. "I don't understand."

Without leaving his seat, Ted pulled a chair from a neighboring table over for the old man. As Dr. Barneveldt sat down, Ted explained, "I got the plane to take off early and fly past its usual dumping spot, so we could seed the area that had to be changed. But I didn't want to tip off the whole fleet of monitoring planes . . . too much of a chance that somebody'd complain and the whole job would get grounded. So, after the seeding plane was on its way, the pilot called back and told the monitoring planes he was off course and was going to dump the pellets and turn back. The monitoring planes never got off the ground."

"So there were no observations made of the experiment?"

"Nope."

"None at all?"

Ted said, "We saw the effect your pellets had on the weather. That's what counts."

Dr. Barneveldt shook his head. "Ted, this is bad science. You have no real data. An experiment should never be run so haphazardly. Suppose there had been no effect on the weather? How would you know what went wrong?"

"Academic question," Ted countered. "When you're

bootlegging, you have to cut corners. You don't make progress without sticking your neck out."

"Behold the lowly turtle," Tuli quipped.

"You are daring," Dr. Barneveldt said. "And lucky."

"We'll see how lucky in a few minutes. Rossman wants to see me at one thirty."

Precisely at 1:30 p.m., Dr. Rossman's secretary ushered the four of us into his office.

He looked up from the paperwork on his desk. "I didn't know this was going to be a group conference."

Right away I could see the clouds darkening: frontal squall.

"We're all involved in this, one way or another," Ted answered.

Rossman eyed us sullenly as we pulled chairs up and sat before his desk.

"I want an explanation of what happened Friday night," he said.

"Simple," Ted said. "We proved that weather control works. And pretty easily, too."

"Don't say 'we,' Marrett!" Rossman snapped. "It's you; keep your friends out of it."

"I'm not looking for protection," Ted shot back. "I'm giving them credit for helping with the basic work."

"But you—and you alone—are responsible for Friday night."

"That's right."

Rossman shuffled through his papers. "Do you know what this is?" He brandished a memorandum. "It's an estimate of the cost to the Department of that plane's flight over the ocean."

"The plane was going to that general region anyway."

"And this," he pulled out a telegram, "is a formal complaint from the Air Force about unauthorized persons being involved in their highly secret laser operations. Unauthorized. That's you, Marrett. You could be cited for a violation of national security!"

"But, Dr. Rossman—" I began.

"Wait a minute, Jerry," Ted said, turning back to Rossman. "Listen. I spent two years in the Air Force, a good chunk of it on orbital duty. I know those lasers inside out. How do you think I got the idea of using 'em to alter the weather? I haven't spied on anybody, or broken Security regs. All I did was ask a buddy of mine who's still on duty up there to pay special attention to a certain geographic location. I didn't even mention the word 'laser' to him. So there's no violation. Don't threaten me."

"Do you realize that I can deduct from your salary the cost of that radiophone call to the orbital station?"

"You can't put radiophone calls through to the military satellites. I went over to Otis Air Force Base—on my own time—and got some friends of mine to place the message."

Rossman glowered at Ted, his long, sour face flushed with anger. "And do you realize that you ruined Dr. Barneveldt's experiment? There weren't even any monitoring planes aloft when the pellets were dropped."

"When are *you* going to realize," Ted demanded, springing to his feet, "that we proved we can change the weather. Efficiently, quickly, and definitely make deliberate changes! You're screaming about nickels and dimes when the whole concept of meteorology can be changed. We can make accurate long-range forecasts; we can understand the planetary flow patterns in detail; *we can change the weather deliber-*

ately. Now are you going to open your eyes or stand there blocking the way?"

Rossman nearly turned purple. Ted stood there before his desk, looming over him. Visibly trembling, Rossman got up from his chair.

"Can you prove you changed the weather?" he asked in a choked voice.

I said, "I can vouch for that, Dr. Rossman. The forecast Saturday morning was completely different from the actual weather."

Ignoring me, he asked Ted again, "Can you prove your illegal operations actually forced a weather change? Or would the change have occurred anyway?"

"We operated. The weather changed. Your own predictions didn't foresee the change."

"But you have no proof whatsoever that the change wasn't completely natural. You made no observations. You took no data. For all you know, the weather would have changed without your lifting a finger."

"No. My long-range forecast showed. . . ."

But Rossman was fishing through the papers on his desk again. "And here's another little item—a note from the statistics group. That rainstorm would have helped alleviate the water shortage that's building up. Suppose the farmers learn that the Climatology Division deliberately took away their best chance for a soaking rain for as far ahead as we can foresee? How long do you think we'd stay in our jobs?"

Ted spread his arms in a gesture of helplessness. "Look, you can't have it both ways. Either we didn't have any effect on the weather or we robbed the pitiful farmers of their rain. Now which is it?"

"I don't know," Rossman snapped. "And I don't care.

Marrett, I will not have people sneaking behind my back. And I will not tolerate insubordination. I'll expect your resignation on my desk by the end of the day. If not, I've got enough on you to get a review board to toss you out on your ear. You're finished, Marrett. Finished!"

7. Cross Currents

I MUST have been in a state of shock as we filed out of Dr. Rossman's office. I really don't remember what we said or did. I can recall Rossman's angry, twisted face, Ted's stunned expression. The next thing I remember is entering my hotel room.

I must have sat there for quite a while. The buzz of the phone snapped my attention to the room around me.

"Answer," I called out, realizing now that the room was dark. Outside, the towers of Back Bay were looming shadows against the reddening sky.

Barney's face took form on the viewscreen. "Jerry . . . what are we going to do? Ted's cleaned out his desk. He's gone."

"Where are you?"

"At Climatology. I . . . what's Ted going to do?"

I could see that she had been crying. "Well, don't go to pieces, now. The world hasn't ended."

Shaking her head, she told me, "You don't understand. Ted is ruined. His career is finished."

"Just because he lost a job? That's not——"

"It's not only a job. The Climatology Division is the only place where Ted had any chance at all of doing the work he wants to do. And Dr. Rossman can prevent him from getting another position anywhere in the Government."

I hadn't realized that. "Well . . . there's private industry. Lots of firms have meteorological offices. My Uncle Lowell's airline, for instance. And they pay a lot better than the Government."

"But they don't do research on weather control . . . or long-range forecasts."

"Maybe they could . . . maybe. . . ."

"And how is Ted going to finish school? The Division was sponsoring him at MIT. Now that he's fired he has no way of paying tuition or anything. And Dr. Rossman won't give him any kind of a reference, and . . . Jerry, it's so hopeless!"

"Wait a minute," I said. "Don't go off the deep end. No matter how bad it looks, we can still figure out something. I remember something my father told me once: When the going gets tough, the tough get going."

She was silent for a moment. I watched her face; it looked like a little girl's, trying to be brave, holding back the tears.

"I just don't think I'm very tough, Jerry," she said. "I just don't know what to do."

All right, a voice inside me said, *talk is easy; now let's see you act.* For the first time in my life, I felt a weight of responsibility settle on me.

"Where is Ted now?" I asked her.

"I don't know. . . . Probably on his way back to his apartment."

"See if you can get him to come here. You come too. And Tuli. We might as well all get together."

"But what are we going to do?"

"I don't know yet," I answered. "But I can tell you what we're *not* going to do: we're not going to mope around and act as if the world's come to a sudden stop."

It was fully dark by the time they got to my room—the three of them together. Ted was gloomy, the first time I'd ever seen him let down.

"Look at 'em," he muttered, standing at my window and watching the crowded, brightly lit streets below. "They walk around with plastic clothes and earplug radios that tell 'em the latest news from the moon. But they've got no more control over the weather than the cavemen did."

He turned to us. "Y'know, when I was a kindergarten kid, my father took me to a movie . . . some cartoon with classical music for a background: *The Sorcerer's Apprentice.* This cartoon character was standing on top of a cliff, making magic, making lightning flash from the clouds, making the sea smash against the base of the cliff. . . . I think that's when I first started wondering about controlling the weather."

He grinned, a little sheepishly. "Kindergarten dream. Pretty wild, eh?"

Barney brought us back to the immediate problem. "Ted, did you talk to the people at MIT?"

With a nod, he answered, "Professor Martingale'll fix it so I can stay and get my degree. I'll be okay, long as I don't overeat between now and June."

"And then what?" I asked.

"Get an instructor's slot at MIT, I guess. Or go back in the Air Force. I won't starve."

"That won't do," Barney said. "You'd never be satisfied teaching freshmen from someone else's textbook."

"Doesn't sound like fun, I'll admit."

He stepped away from the window and sat on the sofa, beside Barney.

"There are a few things I can do," I said. "First off, don't worry about expenses between now and June, Ted. I can take care of that. . . ."

"No," he said firmly. "Thanks Jerry, but nothing doing. I'm not a charity case. Not yet, anyway."

"But. . . ."

"No arguments. From here to June is no sweat. Be tight, but I'll get my degree okay. It's afterward that's the problem."

"You can come to work for Thornton."

"Already thought of that. Thornton's outfits don't do the kind of work I want to do."

"Then we'll start a new office."

"We'll what?"

I was just as surprised as they were. The idea must have been in the back of my mind for several hours, but this was the first moment I had consciously recognized it.

"Sure," I said. "Why not? We'll set up a new Thornton company. Long-range forecasts can be a valuable service. We can make money on it! We'll start our own business, with Thornton backing."

For the first time that evening, Barney looked hopeful. We spent the rest of the night talking over the new idea. It was nearly dawn before we had agreed on the major points. The new company's main product would be long-range forecasts. We wouldn't try to compete with the Weather Bureau's regular forecasting service, but would sell our predictions—for at least two weeks ahead—to private businesses, industrial concerns, and the like.

Most important to Ted, though, was that he would be free to conduct an extensive research program on weather control: that was the *real* objective, the goal we all wanted to reach. Thornton would supply the administrative manpower, the people who would run the office, keep the books, and handle the money. Ted would hire the technical staff, get the long-range forecasting service started, and then concentrate on weather control.

"And the first guy I'm hiring," he said, "is an Oriental kineticist who doubles as the voice of my conscience."

Tuli, sitting cross-legged on the floor in front of the sofa, bowed his head. "I humbly accept the honor . . . depending, of course, on salary and fringe benefits."

I told him, "Don't worry about salaries. Thornton can do a lot better than the Government."

Ted looked at me, a new light on his face. "Hey, I hadn't thought about the money. I can get rich!"

Barney laughed. "Does the pay scale count for computer people, too?"

"No, you're not coming with us," Ted said, shaking his head. "You're staying at Climatology."

She stared at him. "What do you mean?"

"We'll need somebody to keep an eye on the Division . . . especially on Rossman. Got a hunch he won't take kindly to this new company."

"But what can he do about it?" Barney asked.

"Don't know. That's why I want you there to watch him."

Barney didn't argue; she folded her arms and dropped her chin to her chest and pouted.

Ted insisted, "Listen, this is more important than making a social club. We'll still see each other almost every day. And besides, if this idea flops and the company folds, you'll still have a solid job at the Division."

Her stubborn expression remained unchanged.

"You've got your uncle to think about too."

"I can take care of him no matter where I'm working," she said. "I hardly see Uncle Jan during working hours anyway."

Ted ran a hand through his red hair. "Look. Rossman could foul us up in a lot of ways. We need somebody to watch him. You can keep tabs on any special jobs that're being fed into the Climatology computer. Later on, after we get the company rolling and Rossman can't really hurt us, I'll snatch you out of the Division and put you in charge of our computing section. How's that?"

Her frown melted. "I don't have to be in charge of computing . . . I just want to be a part of what you're doing."

"You will be . . . an important part."

"As a spy. All right, I'll do it. But only for a while."

"Okay," Ted said, grinning. "That's enough scheming for one night. Jerry, how soon can you get the ball rolling?"

"I'll talk to my father tomorrow. He'll probably be our first customer. And we'll certainly need his backing. I think I can get my uncles interested in it, too."

"Okay, sooner the better."

"Has anyone considered naming our new company?"

Tuli asked. "An auspicious beginning should include an auspicious name."

"How about 'Marrett and Friends'?" Ted asked, trying to look innocent.

We hooted him down.

Tuli suggested, "Perhaps the title should be quiet and humble, such as 'Weather Studies.' "

"Or 'Weather Dynamics,' " I said.

Ted scowled. "Every twenty-cent company in Massachusetts has the word 'dynamics' in it."

"Why don't we get classical," Barney said, "and look at the Greek roots—Aeolus was the god of the winds. We could name the company something like 'Aeolus Research Laboratory.' "

We mulled it over for a few minutes. Finally Ted nodded. "That's it."

I called Father the next day, and made several calls more as the week wore on. I wanted him to come to Thornton, where we could thrash out the idea firsthand, with Uncle Lowell and Uncle Turner on board as well. He grumbled and groused about it. Finally I got Aunt Louise to invite him to my birthday celebration. There wasn't much of an escape route for him then; he agreed to come.

That Friday night saw a family reunion at Thornton. I asked Ted, Barney, and Tuli to come down the next morning. Friday night was for the Thornton clan. They were all pretty tense when Father arrived, and he was looking rather taut, too. Dinner was polite, but conversation stayed strictly on safe topics—nothing about Grandfather Thorn, or Father's decision to stay in Hawaii and build his own life.

After dinner, in the big living room with the fireplace

large enough to walk into, they started talking about the rocket transports.

"You know," Father said, "this is the first time I've actually ridden in one. They're beautiful. Marvelous flight."

I said, "And with the rockets, Hawaii's just as close to New England as . . . well, New York, really."

"That's right."

Father stared into the flames of the fireplace for a long moment. "You know," he said, "it's good to be back here. I'll have to come more often."

Aunt Louise seemed to reach toward him, even though she hardly moved, physically. "It's very good to have you back again, Richard."

The tension didn't crack completely, but you could feel it go down a notch. It was going to be all right.

The meteorologist's map that night showed a steep pressure gradient across New England, the trailing side of a high-pressure cell that had kept the skies clear and bright. Now it was moving off and warm southwest winds were streaming into the area. There would be plenty of children flying kites tomorrow, he knew.

But to the young musician hurrying across the darkened campus that night, the wind was a wild, living force, warm and mysterious, tossing the newly leafed trees and sighing between him and the stars. It was an emotion, a melody he would try to capture on paper, a memory he would keep for years.

The airline pilot bringing his crowded jet into a landing hated the wind and its sudden gusts. He knew the passengers were blaming him personally for each bump and sickening lurch.

The farm wife sitting on the back porch next to her drowsing husband smiled up at the night wind. It might bring rain. Rain had been scarce. Dryness was powdering the fields, putting worried lines into the sleeping man's face.

Saturday morning Ted and Barney arrived. Tuli stayed in Cambridge to finish some schoolwork. I took them into the library, where Father and his brothers were already sitting around the long table across the room from Grandfather's old desk.

Ted outlined his ideas for Aeolus Research Laboratory, pacing steadily from the table to the big French windows as he spoke. When he finished, there was a moment's silence. Then Uncle Turner said quietly:

"This is a major undertaking you're talking about."

"It's a risk," Lowell agreed. "But what new venture isn't? We can make a tax write-off of it."

"Until we start showing a profit," I said.

Uncle Lowell laughed. "He's got the right attitude."

"I don't know about you two," Father said, "but I need long-range weather forecasts. If you boys can do it, I'll put up a third of the money to get you started."

"What kind of money are we talking about?" Turner asked. "They're going to need a building, staff, computers, experimental equipment—this can get pretty deep."

"Got a list of the equipment and technical staff I want," Ted said, pulling a wad of papers from his pocket. "Been working on it all week."

He put the list on the table and we all hunched over to scan it.

"There's nothing here for the office staff. You'll need personnel men, accounting, purchasing, maintenance. . . ."

Ted shrugged. "I'll handle the technical problems. Administration is something else."

"We'll need a first-rate man to run the business aspects of the lab," I said. "That's important, Ted."

"Okay, but he's got to be in line with the technical work. I won't have a paper shuffler telling the technical staff how to do science."

"Certainly not," Uncle Lowell said.

"Good administrators are hard to come by," Father said.

"Whoever he is, he ought to have a thorough knowledge of the purposes of the laboratory," Uncle Turner said.

"And preferably be closely acquainted with the top technical people," Father added.

Suddenly they were all looking at me.

"Me? Run the business? But I can't. I don't know how . . . I couldn't!"

"Yes, you can," Father said. "And you will."

8. *Aeolus Research*

I DIDN'T argue with Father; that would have been fruitless. And, to tell the truth, I found myself curious to see if I *could* run our little enterprise.

We finished the conference, with my uncles and Father agreeing to finance a year's worth of Aeolus Research's operation. As the meeting broke up and the others walked out of the library, Father held me back.

"I want to tell you something, Jeremy."

He paced slowly to the old desk. As he stood framed there by the big windows, I was startled at how closely he resembled Grandfather. I had never realized it before.

"Jeremy, you're going to be running your own outfit for a while. I wish you every success, but . . . frankly, I think your laboratory will collapse before a year is out."

"What do you mean? We——"

"Now hear me out," he said, raising his hands to quiet me. "Your uncles and I will finance your work for a year and use your long-range forecasts. But what do you think is going to happen during that year?"

Shrugging, I answered, "We'll have to learn how to provide the long-range forecasts at a profit."

He gave me the kind of indulgent chuckle that fathers save for their naïve sons. "Listen to me. Your friend Marrett is going to soak up money like an elephant draining a bathtub. You know that this long-range prediction business is already old hat to him. He's not interested in turning it into a business . . . it's only a means to an end for him. He wants to do research—expensive research on controlling the weather. For every dollar Thornton gives you, he'll be spending six. When we stop paying the bills, you'll go broke in a month."

"I know what's on Ted's mind," I said. "And weather control, when we get it, will be a much bigger business than long-range forecasts."

"If you don't go broke in the meantime."

"Ted can work on a budget." But I didn't say it very loudly.

"Maybe," Father said. "But the temptation of 'free' money from Thornton might ruin him and your laboratory. If you want my advice, you'll spend this year beating the bushes for customers to buy your long-range forecasts. That's the only way to survive after Thornton stops handing you golden eggs."

I nodded.

"And another thing," Father went on. "Sooner or later, Marrett is going to want to do some experimenting. Don't be surprised if you run into some legal troubles with the Government."

"Well, we're expecting Dr. Rossman to try to block us if he gets the chance. But I think——"

"Don't look on this as a personal duel between Rossman and Marrett. I said *legal* problems. Have you ever heard of the Environmental Science Services Administration?"

I shook my head.

"You will. They own the country's air."

"Own the atmosphere?"

"In a sense," Father said, smiling at my confusion. "I did some checking before I left Honolulu. ESSA is the agency that runs all the Government's programs on air pollution, oceanography, mapping, and all types of geophysical research. The Weather Bureau is part of ESSA, you know."

"No, I didn't. . . ."

"Well, for something like the past fifteen years ESSA has had the power to grant or withhold licenses for weather-control experiments. They've turned down quite a few crackpots in that time. Now, what's the difference between cloud seeding and air pollution? It depends on who you ask."

"But they wouldn't refuse a legitimate request. . . ." Then I realized what Father was driving at. "If Dr. Rossman wants to stop us, he could work through ESSA."

Father shrugged. "I don't know; maybe that's what he'll do. I'll bet he's a lot better known at ESSA than your friend Marrett."

I had no answer.

"You're going to have an interesting year, Jeremy," Father said, running a finger along the edge of the old desk. "A very educational year, I believe. I'll expect you back home at the end of it, sadder but wiser, and ready to go to work for an established outfit—Thornton Pacific Enterprises."

"Dredging sea bottoms?"

"It'll look different to you twelve months from now."

I didn't waste time getting Aeolus Research started. I couldn't, not with the memory of Father's patient amusement fresh in my mind.

While Ted was finishing his last six weeks at MIT toward his master's degree, I was shuttling back and forth along the Thornton East Coast offices, recruiting personnel in Boston, Hartford, New York, and Washington. My uncles complained—but laughingly—during weekends at Thornton. Talk of piracy filled the air as I lured some of their junior administrative staff people to Aeolus. But seldom did they refuse me someone I wanted to "steal."

I even made a quick rocket trip back to Honolulu and changed the all-knowing smile on Father's face into a thoughtful frown as I plucked the four best young administrators from Thornton Pacific. I knew Father's people fairly well, and they knew me. A chance to be top men in a brand-new company, instead of waiting years for promotion, was too good for them to turn down.

By the middle of June Aeolus Research had a working front office: administration, finance, personnel, purchasing, maintenance, and me. We also had a technical staff—Ted Marrett and Tuli Noyon.

We found a near-perfect office location at Logan Airport in Boston, where we rented the entire top floor of a four-story building. The Weather Bureau's main Boston station was in the same building, and since their observation equipment was mostly on the roof, their people got to know us very well.

Barney and I schemed up a surprise party for Ted and Tuli when they officially received their degrees. I rented a banquet room at the hotel where I was living while Barney quietly invited everyone Ted knew—which turned out to be most of the Climatology people and seemingly all of MIT.

The party was a smashing success. It was the only time I've ever seen Tuli look shocked. Later, I must have looked the same way. That's when I learned that Ted had promised jobs at Aeolus to practically everyone at the party.

It took a weekend to recuperate. Monday morning, Ted met with me and Paul Cook, Aeolus' personnel manager, in my office at the Laboratory. It was a modest little room: one window that looked out on the airport and harbor, a plain wooden desk, a couch, a few chairs, and some paintings.

"Must be tough living so close to nature," Ted cracked as he plopped himself on the couch. "Danish furniture. Domestic or imported?"

"It came from Sweden," I said. "And the paintings are originals that I happen to like. But if they bother you we can take them off and have the walls painted Climatology gray."

He looked horrified. "Even abstract paintings're better than that!"

"Now that we've settled the decor," Paul said, tapping a foot-high pile of papers on my desk, "how's about getting down to work?"

The personnel manager was the "old man" of our staff—well into his thirties. He was chunky, balding, square-jawed, and outgoing.

"These job applications," he said, "are all from people

who claim to be friends of yours, Teddo. Did you really promise *all* of them positions here?"

Ted raised a cautious eyebrow. "Maybe I was a little too eager. But there're some darned good people in that pile."

"All right," I said. "But we don't want just good people —we want the best. And one of each, at least for the time being."

"Know exactly who I want," Ted said, serious now. "No sweat. I'll get the technical staff set up in a week."

Paul looked relieved. I said, "Good. In two weeks, I'd like to see us get out the first forecasts to our customers."

"Can do," Ted answered.

"And speaking of customers, it'll be important to get as many as we can. We can't depend on Thornton alone."

"That's not a technical job," Ted countered. "I'm here to get the forecasts rolling, and then to do the research. Getting customers is your end of the business."

I had to agree. "Okay. I'll take a crack at bringing in new business."

"Hope you enjoy flying," Paul told me. "You're going to spend a lot of time on jets."

Seeing clouds from the ground is nothing compared to being up in their own domain, flying along with them. Taking off at sunset into a heavy bank of stratus lying thick and gray overhead, climbing into them and watching the world disappear from view, and then bursting out into a sky of flaming red with a royal carpet of deep, soft purple stretching out to the dying sun—nothing on Earth can match that. High in a jet the sky is always clear, no matter what the weather below, except for an occasional wisp of icy cirrus overhead. The sun shines every day up there, the sky is always crystal blue. Far down below, fat clumps of cumulus sail past, casting friendly shadows beneath them, their lumpy tops tufted by invisible tweaking fingers. Lanes and belts of clouds march across the face of the land, and sometimes giant storms blank out everything below and turn the view into an Antarctica of glaring white peaks and hazy valleys. Flying through the clouds, the plane bucks and shudders in their powerful wind currents while their crests whip by the viewport, a curtain of vapor that closes and opens and then closes again to hide even the wings from sight. Towering thunderheads flash ominously, streaking the darkness with lightning. Then the plane lands, back in man's realm of rain and gray, back under the changeable skies, back in the world of weather.

The summer was long and bright. One sun-filled day after another. It was cooler than usual, but still the beach and mountain resorts did record business. Not one weekend was rained out. In fact, except for a few frontal storms, there was hardly any rain to speak of in New England. No one complained except the farmers. It was too dry, the crops were withering. But everyone in the cities knew that the autumn rains would solve the problem. Suburban home-owners sprinkled their lawns to keep them green, and talked about the salt-water conversion plants that had made water shortages a thing of the past.

But despite the desalting plants, the northeastern corner of the country was caught in a drought.

And so was I.

That whole summer, no matter where I traveled and how hard I worked, I couldn't uncover a single new customer for Aeolus Research's long-range weather forecasts.

"It looks fine on paper," said the manager of a canned-goods firm, "and we would certainly be interested in predictions that could help us tell exactly when to plant each crop, and how much rainfall to expect. But if this scheme gave us some *wrong* information, we could ruin a year's crop. Besides, why isn't the Weather Bureau using this idea, if it's so good?"

Another businessman was more blunt. "I don't deal with people I don't know. I know the Government weather people. I don't know you. Or your ideas."

In Kansas City, the president of an international hotel chain told me, "It looks great, it really does. Like a dream come true. But those buzzards on the board of directors just won't believe it. They'd never be the first to try something new."

And the chief scientist of an oil company snorted, "Nonsense! The scheme will never work. And I know, because I'm a trained geologist!"

"What's geology got to do with it?" Ted exploded when I told him about that one.

I was slumped in my office chair, gazing forlornly out the window at the gray September sky. Ted paced across the carpeting endlessly.

"Didn't you show 'em the forecasts we've been supplying for Thornton?"

Nodding, I answered, "It didn't convince them. It's only about twelve weeks' worth of predictions, and they claim that either we're lucky or . . . or we're cheating, writing the forecasts after seeing the Weather Bureau's."

"What?" He stiffened, eyes blazing. "Who said that?"

"A couple of them. Not in so many words, but their meaning was clear enough."

ELTING MEMORIAL LIBRARY
93 MAIN STREET
NEW PALTZ, N. Y.

Ted grumbled something to himself.

"Don't be sore at them," I said. "It's my fault. I couldn't convince them."

Ted paced and muttered for a few minutes more. I stayed slumped in my chair. I had just returned from a cross-country flight and hadn't slept more than six hours in the previous two days.

"Listen," he said, pulling up a chair beside my desk. "Maybe you were talking to the wrong guys. Instead of aiming at the company presidents and research directors, you ought to be talking to the working-level engineers and group leaders . . . the guys who'd use our forecasts if their bosses'd buy 'em. The stuffed shirts up at the top know what's impossible; nobody can convince 'em in one sitting. But get to the plant managers or research scientists or engineers. Invite 'em here to the Lab; pay their way if you have to. Let 'em spend a few days here, learning what we do and how we do it. Then they'll be on our side."

"And then they'll convince their own bosses?"

"Right."

"Do you think it'll work . . . in time, I mean. We've only got until next April."

He grinned. "It'd better work!"

The winter came and went, colder, more severe than usual, but with comparatively little snow. The skiers complained bitterly, and several mountain resorts closed for long stretches while their owners sadly contemplated bare slopes and melting bank accounts. In February, a good part of Boston harbor froze over and the Coast Guard had to assign an icebreaker to keep the port partially open. Back away from the coast, in the frigid valleys and frozen hill-sides, the farmers waited stonily for the snow that never came. Not enough spring runoff from the mountains, they knew. The streams would be shallow in the spring; the fields would be dry.

9. Drought Pattern

During that bitter, dry winter, I followed Ted's strategy. It took an endless amount of travel and talking, living in strange hotel rooms, eating in all sorts of restaurants, waking in the mornings and straining hard to recall which city and what day of the week it was. But the young engineers and researchers started trickling in to the Laboratory. One or two at a time, they'd come in for a few days, watch and listen to Ted and Tuli, and go back to their jobs with new lights in their eyes. By March we were getting official inquiries from several companies. They wanted to do business with us.

The meteoroid was a chunk of rock no bigger than a man's fist. For thousands of centuries it had orbited about the sun without coming to within twenty million miles of another solid body its own size. But at an inevitable point in time, the far-distant sun and planets aligned themselves in such a way that the meteoroid was pulled to within a few million miles of Earth. It was close enough. Earth's powerful gravity drew the little rock; it gained speed and began "falling" toward the blue planet. It hit the atmosphere going about twelve miles per second and formed a shock wave that heated the air around it to incandescence. The rock itself began to boil away; by the time it had plunged to within twenty-five miles of Earth's surface there was nothing left of it but a fine spray of microscopic dust grains. For days the dust sifted downward. Some of the grains glided over the American Midwest and were washed out of the air by rainfall. Part of the meteoroid's substance reached the ground in raindrops and eventually flowed to sea. But over New England, the dust grains drifted through the air for days. Conditions seemed good for rain: there was moisture in the air, and dust nuclei; the winds were coming off the ocean. But no rain fell.

"So you managed to get through a year without folding up," Father said. He looked pleased and puzzled at the same time, as I watched him on my office viewscreen.

"You seem surprised," I said.

"I am."

Leaning back in my swivel chair and clasping my hands behind my head, I admitted, "So am I . . . a little."

"The long-range forecasts have been very accurate," Father said. "This spring has been just as rough as last year's, but the dredging is going smoothly. We'll even be able to recoup what we lost last spring."

"Ted worked very hard on those forecasts."

Father chuckled. "He hasn't driven you broke yet?"

"Not yet. He's tried a few times, but we've been able to hold the line, so far. He's got the forecasts coming out for two weeks ahead now. I wanted him to extend them to four weeks, but he drew the line there. He's putting all his efforts and budget into research on weather control."

"A four-week forecast would be very valuable."

"I know. But Ted's made up his mind. We have the two-week forecasts and the ninety-day general climatological predictions . . . you know, they predict the average temperatures and rainfall for a given area, and show the storm tracks."

"Yes, I've seen them. They're good."

I nodded. "Well, we get the two-week forecasts out every Wednesday; that gives us overlapping coverage. And the ninety-day predictions come out once a month. To do more than that, we'd need more technical staff, which we can't afford yet. Ted's got a small crew working on nothing but research, of course."

"Of course."

"Don't think he's locked himself in some ivory tower, Dad. Whenever we've had trouble with the forecasts, he's dropped the research to help straighten things out. And he's spent a lot of time showing potential customers what we can do for them. He's our all-star team, all in one man."

"It sounds as if you're in reasonably good shape, then." Father looked almost happy about it.

"We're afloat. We've signed up four new customers, besides the Thornton concerns, and three other companies are talking about contracts with us."

"Good. You've got the company on its feet. Your friends are gainfully employed. You've had a year's worth of experience . . . and fun. Now I want you to come back home, son. I need you here."

"Home?" I snapped forward in the chair and grabbed the desk hard with both hands. "But I never . . ."

"Thornton Pacific is your company, Jeremy. Not this weather business."

"You can't expect me to just walk out of here!"

"I certainly can," he said firmly. "I want you back home where you belong."

"I can't leave now."

"You mean you won't!"

"Are you *ordering* me to come home?"

"Is that what you want me to do?"

By now I was sitting on the front inch of my chair. Father and I were glaring at each other.

"Listen, Dad. The first Jeremy Thorn put his money into clipper ships when all his advisers and friends were backing the Erie Canal. Grandfather—Jeremy the Second—put the family into the airplane business. You yourself marched off to Hawaii and went into the undersea business. All right— I'm following the family pattern. I'm sticking here and weather control is what I'm after."

"But it's impossible."

"So were airplanes and deep-sea dredges."

"All right!" he shouted. "Be a stubborn little idiot. But don't think you can come running home to safety when your pipe dreams fall flat! You're on your own, don't ask me for help or advice."

"Isn't that the same speech Grandfather made to you before you went to Hawaii?"

He snapped off the connection. The screen went dead. I was on my own.

And enjoying it! I had never really worked before starting Aeolus, never really sunk my teeth into a job that just wouldn't get done unless I did it. Now I was working night and day. I spent more time in my office than in my hotel room. I forgot about TV, and sailing, and even visiting

Thornton. But I don't think I've ever had as much fun, as much of a feeling of *building* something worthwhile, as I did when we were getting Aeolus into high gear.

Late one night, a week or so after Father's explosion, Ted popped into my office.

"Still working?"

I looked up from the contract I was trying to read. "There's a lot of fine print to wade through in this job."

"Got a friend of yours outside. Took her to dinner and she wanted to come over and say hello. Hasn't seen much of you the past couple of weeks."

"Barney? Where is she?"

"Down in my shop, with Tuli."

"Tuli's still here? What's going on tonight?"

Ted leaned nonchalantly against the doorjamb, his big frame filling the open doorway. "Been doing some calculations about the drought. Barney's checking 'em over."

I closed the contract folder and shoved it into a desk-top basket.

"This must be pretty special," I said, getting to my feet. "You could have used the regular Aeolus computations group to check your calculations."

"Already did. Barney's double-checking . . . and seeing if Rossman's done anything along the same lines."

We walked down the hall to Ted's room. He didn't have a regular office; his room was big enough to hold a squash court. He had all sorts of junk in it: a desk with a table to one side of it and an electronics console on the other, half a dozen file cabinets, a tattered old contour lounge that he had somehow smuggled out of the Air Force, a conference table surrounded by the unlikeliest assortment of chairs, and no less than four coffeepots standing in a row on the windowsill. Outside the window was a small automatic weather station.

The entire wall opposite the door was covered by Ted's private joy: a viewscreen map of the continental United States. He had worked nonstop for weeks to make the map exactly the way he wanted it.

Barney and Tuli were sitting at the conference table as we walked in, thumbing through sheets of notes that were partly computer print-out and partly Ted's heavy-handed scrawl.

She looked up as we entered. "Jerry, how are you?"

"I'm fine. How have you been?"

"She's obviously in wonderful shape," Ted cracked. "Now, what about the numbers, Barney?"

"I can't find anything glaringly wrong with them," she said with a shrug. "Of course, I haven't had time really to go through it thoroughly. . . ."

"Could use our computer," Ted suggested.

Tuli said in that quiet way of his, "The computer runs at any hour of the day or night. It's entirely free of human frailty, such as the need for sleep."

"All right, so I'm asking a favor," Ted said, waving his hands. "I'd feel better about the numbers if Barney checked 'em out."

"Can I start tomorrow night?" she asked.

"After dinner," I said.

"Okay, we'll all eat together," Ted countered.

I asked, "What is this all about, anyway?"

Instead of answering, Ted paced to the console beside his desk and touched a few buttons. A weather map sprang up on the lighted viewscreen: lines and symbols that showed air masses and storm cells across the country, and the weather reported at each major city.

"Here's the way it looks right now," Ted said. "Those numbers down in the bottom right corner are precipitation totals from New England. So far this year, we're standing at nearly half the region's average rainfall."

"And snowfall," Tuli added softly.

"That pile of calculations I showed you," Ted went on, squatting on his desk, "is a general forecast for New England as far ahead as I can make halfway accurate numbers. Runs to the end of the year."

"Seven months," Barney mused. "The reliability won't be terribly high. . . ."

"Maybe not, but take a look." Ted fiddled with the control buttons, and we watched the weather patterns unfold across the face of the continent. Hot summer air welled up from the tropics, late-afternoon thunderstorm symbols flickered here and there, cooler air masses swung in from the north and west, triggering squall lines across their fronts. You could see autumn taking hold of the nation, and hurricanes hitting Florida and the Gulf Coast. Then came winter and bitter Arctic air, with tiny starlike symbols of snow sprinkling over the northern two-thirds of the country.

"It's now December thirty-first," Ted said when the map stopped changing. "Happy New Year."

"Not very happy," Tuli observed, "if those precipitation figures are correct."

I looked at the numbers; New England had received less than half of its usual rainfall.

"Drought pattern," Ted said. "And a rough one. This neck of the country's in for trouble. While the Midwest'll be flooded."

"What are you going to do about it?" Barney asked.

"Stop it."

"How?"

"Don't know . . . yet. But I'm going to make it the business of this Lab to find out."

Turning from the map toward Ted, I said, "We'll have to find considerably more money to work on a problem of this size."

"We're going to work on it," Ted answered firmly. "You can worry about the money. If you can find people who want to pay us for it, great. But we're going to work on it anyway."

He turned to Barney. "Rossman doing anything like this?"

"Not that I know of. Of course, his official forecasts don't run this far into the future."

"But unofficially?"

"I think he's trying to figure out your type of forecasting technique. He has a small group of people doing some special work for him. It's very hush-hush. At least, no one will tell me anything about it."

Ted didn't answer, but his face settled into a frown.

That night I took the slideway home to my hotel. It was a beautiful warm night, with the thinnest sliver of a moon in a cloudless, star-studded sky. I found myself wishing it would rain.

While Ted was studying the drought pattern, I decided to take a look at the political climate of New England. I found that most of the people in the governments of the six states considered the drought bothersome, but not really serious. No one seemed terribly worried; the salt-water conversion plants were preventing any real shortages in the coastal cities, and the inland reservoirs were still in fairly good shape.

But there was going to be a meeting of the Resources Managers of the New England States, one of a series of regional meetings for various departments of the state governments. This one was for the people who worry about natural resources . . . such as water.

I cornered Ted in Tuli's kinetics lab and told him about it. "It's going to be over the Fourth of July weekend."

"Foul up the weekend to talk to a bunch of bureaucrats?" He was plainly disgusted.

"To talk," I replied, "with the people who'll buy drought alleviation . . . if you can sell it."

"*If* I can sell it? Insults yet! Okay bossman, you want fireworks for the Glorious Fourth, you'll get 'em."

It took some string-pulling to get us on the conference agenda. I finally had to talk to a Congressman from Lynn; he was on the House of Representatives' Science and Natural Resources Committee, and was helping to make the arrangements for the meeting.

The biggest job was getting Ted prepared to speak to a group of non-meteorologists. The first time he rehearsed his talk he spent fifty minutes showing slides and explaining the science of meteorology. We all tried to argue him out of it.

"It's got to be simplified," I insisted. "These people don't understand meteorology. I couldn't even follow most of your talk."

He sat on the couch in my office and folded his arms

like a stubborn little boy. "What do you want me to do, tell 'em fairy tales?"

"Right! Exactly right," I said. "Tell them a fairy tale . . . a horror story. Show them how bad this drought's going to be. And then show them enough to convince them that you can break it up."

"Is that fair?" Tuli asked.

"If you're talking to people who don't understand the nature of the problem," Barney said, "you've got to speak in language that will get through to them."

"Okay," Ted said with a shrug. "The talk'll be show business, not science."

Take the energy of a full-fledged storm and compress it into a narrow funnel so that its wind speed reaches five hundred knots, causing a semi-vacuum inside its rotary structure. Such winds hit a wall with a force of a thousand pounds per square foot. And the vacuum immediately behind the wind makes the normal air pressure in a building explode the walls outward. Such a funnel makes a fine weapon, especially in a crowded city. It is called a tornado.

It was a gray, soggy afternoon in Tulsa, with thick bulbous clouds hanging low. The weather map showed a strong cold front approaching from the northwest, pushing into oppressively humid tropical air. A tornado alert had been issued by the Weather Bureau, and planes were seeding some of the clouds, trying to disperse them before danger struck. The shopping center was jammed nonetheless; tomorrow, the Fourth, stores would be closed. The funnel dropped out of the clouds suddenly, hissing and writhing like a supergiant snake, spewing lightning. It touched a pond and instantly sucked it dry, hopped over a parking lot, and pounced on the main shopping buildings. They exploded. It was all over in thirty seconds. Forty-two killed, more than a hundred injured. The funnel disappeared, and soon after the clouds blew away. The sun shone down on five acres of sheer devastation.

Ted and I saw the results of the tornado on the TV news as we 'coptered out to the meeting on the morning of the Fourth.

"Instead of taking a chance on weather control," he muttered, gesturing toward the wreckage shown on the TV screen, "they'd rather sit back and let *that* happen."

The conference was taking place in a resort hotel in the Berkshire Mountains. We flew over lovely wooded hills and rolling farmlands. As we went farther west, though, more and more brown patches were sprinkled in among the green. The lakes and ponds were shrinking; we could see the muddy, rocky edges that were normally under water.

"Dry streambed," Ted pointed out to me. "And there's another."

"It looks pretty serious," I said, looking at the sandy gullies that had been streams.

"This is nothing. Wait another couple of months. And *next* summer'll be a beaut."

"But your forecasts don't go that far."

"This kind of pattern runs four to five years before it changes, unless something kinky happens . . . like weather control."

The hotel was swarming with conference members. They had come from all six New England states, from New York, and from Washington. We arrived just before lunch, in time for the brief outdoor ceremony in honor of the Fourth.

As we elbowed our way through the crowd to one of the hotel's four restaurants, Ted grumbled, "More politicians here than I've ever seen under one roof."

We ate quickly and then got one of the hotel's assistant managers to show us to the conference room where we were scheduled to speak. It was a small, windowless room, with a slide projector set up at one end and a projection screen at the other.

"Got here early," Ted said as the manager shut the door behind him. "Nobody's here."

"I'll put your slides in the projector," I said.

I was putting the last slide in when the door opened and a man in his middle thirties stepped into the room.

"I'm Jim Dennis," he said, extending his hand to us.

Congressman Dennis had a round pleasant face, slightly ruddy, with a slow smile and eyes that seemed to look well past the surface of things. He was about my own height, and of medium build.

"Why's a Congressman from Lynn worrying about the drought?" Ted asked. "Lynn's got a desalting plant."

Dennis thought a moment before answering. "I wouldn't say I'm worried, exactly—I'm concerned. I'm on the House Science Committee. We've been hearing some grumblings about the drought, but the experts have been telling us there's no problem, no problem at all. They've been saying it louder and louder the past month or so. Now it seems you boys think there *is* a problem."

"Don't trust the experts?" Ted jabbed.

Dennis smiled. "Not when they all agree."

Within a few minutes our audience started arriving. Congressman Dennis knew all of them by name and introduced us as they came in. By the time we started, there were eleven men sitting around the conference table. They all came from the agricultural departments of the New England states, except for one representative of the Boston Weather Bureau office, a Mr. Arnold.

Must be somebody new, Ted scribbled on a pad for me to read. *Never saw him at Climatology.*

After they were all seated, Ted launched into his talk. His slides were mainly photos of the big viewscreen map at Aeolus, picturing how the drought would remain and worsen for the rest of the year.

"And we're still on the downslide," he summarized. "The drought hasn't reached bottom yet; there's worse to come."

"Now wait a minute," Arnold said. He was spare, sharp-featured, with thinning hair combed over his bald spots.

Ted flicked off the slide projector and the room lights came up.

"Just how much faith can we put in these forecasts?" Arnold demanded. "Six months ahead is much too far to draw concrete conclusions."

"Half a dozen top business firms're buying our long-range predictions. And even though the forecasts for six months ahead aren't as reliable as our two-week forecasts, they still show the general trend. The drought's going to be with us for a long time."

"There's a big difference between two weeks and six months."

Ted walked slowly down to the meteorologist's chair, his face reddening. Before he could say anything, I jumped in.

"I think our forecasting method is much more detailed than the Weather Bureau's, so even a six-month forecast will be considerably more accurate than you might suspect at first glance."

Ted, looming over Mr. Arnold, added in a barely controlled voice, "Monday morning I'll send each of you our regular weekly forecast. It'll predict pinpoint weather conditions, hour by hour, for every section of New England for the next fourteen days. Compare it with any other forecast you want to—there's nothing as accurate or as detailed."

"This is all beside the point," one of the others said. "I don't see where the drought can really hurt us. After all, we have the desalting plants . . . there's no water shortage, we have the whole ocean to draw from."

"That's all right for you in Rhode Island," the man next to him said. "One desalting plant covers all your needs. But in New Hampshire we're already feeling the pinch. Dairy farms and some industrial plants are complaining about poor-quality water and some actual shortages."

"Same thing here in Western Massachusetts," agreed the man across from them. Gesturing with a long cigar, he added, "According to the people in Washington, we couldn't get another desalting plant built in less than two years. By then the damage will have been done."

"But this is all a matter of control and conservation, isn't it?" the Rhode Islander countered. "There's plenty of water to go 'round. You've just got to stop wasting it."

Congressman Dennis objected. "People have been working on water conservation for years, and some very good steps have been taken. We're doing about as well in that respect as you can expect, and certainly we're not going to do much better overnight. The problem is that there may not be enough water available, if Mr. Marrett is right and the drought continues."

"We still use only about seven percent of the rain that actually falls," Arnold said. "The rest goes off to the sea."

"That may be true," Dennis agreed calmly, "but it's the best we can do right now."

Ted walked back to the head of the table. "Let's face facts. All the work you've put into water management and pollution control has been more than matched by growing population and industry. You've been running as hard as you can just to stay abreast of the problem. Now the drought's going to knock your legs out from under you. Unless something changes darned soon, you're going to go on water rationing."

"We could lose billions of dollars . . . farm products, industrial output. . . ."

"Not to mention our jobs," someone muttered.

"Then you've got to act!" Ted snapped. They all jolted to attention and looked at him. "We can break up this drought. We can end it, by making deliberate, controlled changes in the weather."

Now they looked at each other and started murmuring.

"If you mean cloud seeding, that's been tried and——"

"There's no sense seeding clouds when the conditions aren't right," Ted answered. "I'm talking about making the conditions what we want them to be, so rain'll fall naturally. Weather *control* . . . breaking the drought pattern."

"But if there's no moisture in the air, how——"

"Listen. There's six times more water moving over our heads right now than there is in all the lakes and streams of New England. All we have to do is bring it down here where we need it."

"Can you do that?"

"We can make the long-range weather forecasts. We

have chemicals and energy sources for changing the weather. We can predict what the changes'll be, so that we can tell beforehand if they'll do harm or good."

"Have you really done any of this?"

"Not on the scale that'll be needed for breaking the drought, no."

"But on any scale at all? Has it been done?"

Ted glanced at me and grinned. "If it hadn't been, we wouldn't be here now."

"And just how do you expect to break the drought?" Arnold asked, with a hint of acid in his tone.

"If I knew the answers I'd be out doing the job. But I know how to get the answers."

"How?"

Ted ticked off on his fingers. "First, do a theoretical study of the conditions necessary for normal rainfall. This'll be partly a historical study of past records to see what the normal patterns are, from the ground up to the ionosphere. At the same time we'll run computer models of large-scale weather patterns to see how they affect the New England situation."

"Large scale?"

"Planetary patterns . . . northern hemisphere, mostly."

Their eyes widened, but they kept listening.

"Second: after we've got a handle on the conditions you need for normal rainfall, we'll compare 'em with this drought condition. Then we'll set up some lab experiments and computer simulations to see if we can make simple changes to the weather that'll trigger the lasting kind of change we want."

He looked around the table to see if they were following

him. "The atmosphere's like one of those children's humpty-dumpty toys. It resists change. Has tremendous powers of equilibrium. Hit it from one side and it'll just rock back and forth until it comes back to where it started."

"But it does change," one of the men said.

"Sure! Weather changes minute to minute, and climate changes too—like this drought. But climate changes are slow and involve huge gobs of energy. We can't compete with the natural energy balances in the atmosphere . . . they're too big and we're too little. It'd be like a man going against a mammoth."

Congressman Dennis chuckled. "Men slaughtered the mammoths."

"Right," Ted agreed. "But not with muscles. With brains."

"What are you driving at?" Arnold demanded.

"Just this: we've got to look for natural situations in the drought pattern where we can tip the scales a little and swing big changes in our favor. We can't force the atmosphere to change completely against its natural balance . . . but we can find chances to trigger the change we want with just a little nudge at the right time and place."

"One or two simple modifications won't change a pattern as deeply impressed as this one," Arnold said.

"Maybe not. But in the lab we can take a look at all the possible changes we can make. And with these long-range forecasts we can see which changes'll break up the drought, and then go out and make 'em."

"Pie in the sky," Arnold said. "You can't go around tinkering with the weather and——"

"Not tinkering!" Ted snapped. "We'll be running controlled experiments, based on theoretical predictions and computer simulations. Same way engineers design airplanes and rockets."

He leaned his big fists on the table and said to them, "Instead of just watching the drought ruin us, I want to see human intelligence put to work to stop it. We don't have to sit around and wait for nature to run its course, any more than a sick man has to go without medicine. We can break this drought. Let's do it."

10. Competition

THE committee seemed impressed by Ted's speech, and several of the men promised to look into our drought-alleviation idea. But the following Monday morning, back at Aeolus, Ted was gloomy.

"Same old story," he grumbled. "Don't call us, we'll call you."

When I came back to my office after lunch, though, a call from Congressman Dennis was waiting for me.

"I got your forecast this morning," he said, holding up the photoprinted copy for me to see. "It looks very impressive."

"Thanks. We like to think it is."

"I took the liberty of calling a few friends here and there," he went on, with a knowing grin. "Do you realize that it really did rain this morning in Sherman Mills, Maine? And the fog you predicted along the Connecticut Turnpike came and went on schedule, just as you predicted?"

I hadn't read the forecast in detail, so I merely smiled and nodded.

"According to the date on this copy," Dennis went on, "these predictions were issued last Wednesday."

"Yes, we send out that type on Wednesdays. The forecast was actually made almost a week ago."

"I had lunch with the Governor this noontime, at the State House, and I showed him your predictions. He was interested."

"Oh? How interested?"

Dennis let me hang in suspense for a moment. Then, "Well, I had phoned him about Ted's talk on the drought and weather control. He asked me over for lunch to discuss it further. I think the next step is for you people to see him."

"Wait a minute," I said. "I want to get Ted into this."

I buzzed the switchboard and they connected Ted's phone to the line. I still saw only Dennis' face on the viewscreen, but I could hear Ted's voice as Dennis explained the Governor's interest.

"Now we can *really* get to work," Ted beamed. "Tell the Governor he's a far-sighted statesman."

Dennis laughed. "He won't believe that. Besides, he only wants to do some talking; he hasn't signed a contract with you yet."

"He will," Ted answered, "if he wants the drought broken."

Ted signed off, and I thanked the Congressman for his help.

He leaned a little closer to the viewscreen and said in a confidential whisper, "Don't thank me. Politicians are always looking for something good to hitch their wagons to. Weather control might make me a Senator some day."

"I certainly hope so," I said.

"So do my five kids!"

It took several conferences at the State House, and an inspection tour of Aeolus by the Governor and his staff, but by mid-October we had a contract with the Commonwealth of Massachusetts to study methods of alleviating the drought. By the end of the month the five other New England states had given us similar contracts. We plunged into a whirlwind of work. Ted hired additional scientific staffers, and split the staff into two distinct groups: one for turning out the forecasts, and the other concentrating completely on the drought. For the first time since Aeolus Research opened up, I could stop looking for new business; we had more than we could handle. Even the Environmental Science Services Administration came in with a small contract. ESSA wanted to coordinate our work with other studies being done by various Government agencies, mainly in the fields of water conservation and management.

It was a dry, brittle autumn, without the coastal storms of normal years. Frosts came early and then a flood of southern air swept into New England. Indian summer, but not a pleasant one. Cool air from the north was trapped under the lighter, warmer air. Meteorologists called it a thermal inversion. For days on end the weather was deathly calm, without even a breeze to rustle the paper-dry colored leaves. The air hung heavy with smoke and fog from burning leaves, tinderbox forests ablaze, automobile exhausts, factory smokestacks, sea fog along the coasts—all blended into a hazy, sickening smog that crawled over the landscape and settled down, with no wind to blow it away. Straight overhead the sky was clear and heart-catchingly blue; but the horizon was lost in dirty mists. Respiratory ailments soared upward sharply, eyes stung and watered, breathing was difficult for many. Indian summer, the best season of all in normal times. Now everyone looked for cold, and snow, and above all, wind.

Indian summer ended in a single day when a thirty-knot wind howled down from the northwest and sent thermometers plummeting all over New England. It was winter, sudden, sharp, and painfully cold.

The months rattled by one after the other. Ted drove himself night and day, working on the drought problem. He wore out whole sets of assistants, computers, and researchers. Tuli kept up with him most of the time, but only by taking a three- or four-day break each month to do nothing but rest. Ted never rested. I had my hands full with business matters, especially getting out progress reports to keep our new customers happy. Research results, financial status, equipment purchased, papers written, personnel hired, consultants, travel, material—we had to report on everything.

Straight through the winter Ted hammered on the theoretical side of the problem. He was trying to uncover the causes of the drought, the reasons why a climate pattern so unlike the usual one can establish itself over the area for years on end. Part of this search, of course, was devoted to identifying the conditions needed to break the drought.

"Breaks up by itself sooner or later," he mused in one of the rare moments we had to talk together. "Got to get three basic patterns: the drought pattern, the normal pattern, and the changeover where the drought starts to break up."

"And once you've identified all three?"

He waved a hand. "Then we start to worry about how to move the drought through a break-up pattern into the normal situation. But first we've got to get the parameters of each one down in black and white. Which ain't easy, friend."

It was a staggering computer job. Millions upon millions of bits of data were fed into the computers in an attempt to make some understandable sense out of the known weather conditions, past and present. Not only the conditions for New England had to be accounted for; the entire northern hemisphere was put into the picture.

"Drought's only one small slice of the global picture," Ted pointed out. "Can't play blind men and the elephant. Got to see the whole beast—with both eyes wide open."

It was too big a job for Aeolus' computers to handle alone. I tried to get help from the local Weather Bureau, but they turned me down. ESSA in Washington did the same; not a single agency would cooperate with us.

"Rossman's work," Ted growled.

So I turned to Thornton, while Ted tried persuading MIT. We spent a medium-sized fortune setting up a tight-beam microwave communications link over half the eastern seaboard so that computers from Thornton's Washington, New York, and Boston offices and the MIT computers could "talk" with our own machines at our Logan Airport location. The effect was to produce a computer of prodigious size and ability; a few hundred miles between the various parts of our super-computer meant nothing to the machine. It worked with the speed of light. Literally.

By the time the next Fourth of July came by, the drought was major news. The year before, only a few specialists had been concerned. Now there were stories in all the news media and on television almost every day. Reservoirs had dried up, streams had disappeared, even large rivers were showing sandbars and boulders where no living person could remember anything but deep, moving water. Farm delegations were angrily clamoring for action, and we had to keep Ted carefully away from newsmen for fear that he'd give the impression we could break up the drought in a few weeks. Our official line was that we were carrying out research, but the final answers might be years away.

Inland cities went on water rationing that summer, and factories began closing down, throwing thousands out of work. The coastal cities fared better with their desalting plants, but even there they couldn't make enough fresh water to come close to the demands for it. Suburban lawns began to wither and wells went dry under the uninterrupted blaze of the summer sun. Public fountains were turned off, air conditioners went out unless they used no water, fishing and camping grounds were closed against the threat of forest fires.

But in the Midwest rivers swelled over their banks to flood cities and farms alike under a merciless series of torrential downpours.

By midsummer Ted was ready for experiments. Most of them were down in the lab, but for some we rented planes and ran tests far out at sea. We had to keep very quiet about the experiments, for fear the press would make the public think that the problem would be solved with a wave of Ted's hand.

About the only time I saw Barney all that summer, for more than a quick hello or a hurried meal together, was in

August when the Perseid meteor shower put on its annual show.

The shower was at its height over a weekend, and I brought her down to Thornton where we could get a good view of the sky from the beach.

We stayed on the beach all night, watching the meteors burn across the sky, streaks of light against the changeless stars. They came from all quarters, flashing into brilliance, some of them showering sparks as they raced across the heavens and then snuffed out, all in the span of a heartbeat. If you traced their courses backward, they all tracked to the constellation Perseus, the Hero.

Somehow they reminded me of Ted, these meteors that made the stars themselves seem commonplace as they dashed through the sky, brilliant, purposeful, following a trail that never wavered. They moved in absolute silence, an eerie contrast to their blazing luminosity. It was as if they knew exactly where they had to go, and were hurrying to take their assigned places before some celestial deadline fell.

For hours our conversation was limited to brief snatches about the meteors. There was just too much going on overhead to think of anything else. But finally the sky began to pale and the meteors slacked off. Somewhere up near the house I could hear a bird start to twitter. The stars were fading out, and the sea horizon was beginning to turn pink.

We walked, suddenly sleepy now, back to the house.

"How is Ted?" Barney asked.

"Haven't you seen him?"

She shook her head. "Not for a week or so."

"He's all right," I said. "Working like a demon. Make that two demons."

"Uncle Jan said he's possessed . . . possessed by the idea of controlling the weather."

"But why? Why should someone get so wrapped up in an idea?"

She stopped and turned back to look at the brightening eastern sky. "I don't know. Maybe he's afraid that there's nothing else he can do that amounts to anything important. Whatever it is, it could destroy him. If it doesn't work—or if he's kept from making it work—it could tear him apart."

"I guess so, but everything seems to be going pretty well," I said.

"I'm afraid for him, Jerry. Something's going on at Climatology. I'm not sure what it is, they won't let me get close to it. Dr. Rossman has a special group working off by themselves. They've even commandeered a section of our computers, and no one else can go near them."

"Could mean trouble."

She agreed with an unhappy little nod. "Dr. Rossman has made several trips to Washington the past week. I think he's talking to people in the Environmental Science Services Administration."

"ESSA? Who's he talking to there?"

"I'm not sure. His secretary let something slip about the licensing group, but I couldn't figure out what she meant."

11. Breakup

TED was furious about Barney's news.

"Just like him!" he shouted in my office that Monday morning. "He can't figure out what we're doing so he's down to Washington, trying to slow us." He kept pounding his fist into his palm as he stalked up and down in front of my desk.

"It sounds as if he's pulling some important wires," I said.

Ted stopped and glared at me. "Pulling wires, is he? Let's see if he's got a wire as good as this one."

He stamped out of the office. I scrambled out of my chair and went after him. Half running, I followed him down the corridor to his workroom. Tuli and three other staff members were locked deep in conversation when we entered:

"Hold it, here's the boss," one of them said.

I didn't know if they meant Ted or me.

"One of you guys work the viewscreen controls," Ted ordered as he went to the big viewscreen map. Tuli went to the desk as Ted picked up an arrow-beam flashlight pointer. "Okay, run it back to the standard pattern."

The weather symbols on the big map disappeared briefly as Tuli touched the control studs on the console. Then a pattern of colored arrows took form on the map. Ted stood unmoving for a moment, still obviously steaming, trying to force self-control on himself.

Finally he said, "This is the usual wind pattern for the continental United States during the summer." Pointing with the flashlight, he explained, "Jet stream comes in over the West Coast, dips south, and then swings northeast. Cold air, these blue arrows, comes down from Canada, gets into the westerly stream and slants out toward the Atlantic."

He glanced at me to see if I was getting it. I nodded. "Red arrows show maritime tropical air coming up from the Gulf of Mexico and the Caribbean, up along the East Coast. That's rainmaking air for us."

He gestured to Tuli, who flicked another set of buttons.

"Now see this high-pressure ridge sitting out over the ocean? It's up at high altitudes. Position moves around a little but it's usually not far from the shore. High-altitude air flows northward along the west side of the ridge— clockwise motion around a High—up from the tropical seas and along the East Coast."

"That's what guides the rainmaking air toward New England," I guessed.

"Check. Now look at the drought pattern."

Tuli made the map symbols shift and change. The high-pressure ridge moved westward, inland, and settled approximately around the Appalachian mountain chain. The jet stream curved on a more southerly route. And the red arrows of rainy air moved only halfway up the East Coast, then split; one branch swung out to sea, the other moved into the Midwestern states.

Ted, slowly forgetting Rossman in his concentration on the meteorology, was cooling off. "Now look. The high-pressure ridge moves inland, and sucks the maritime air into the Midwest, mostly. New England gets cut off from it. And worse, now there's cool dry air coming down the eastern side of the ridge, right into New England. Even when we do get moisture, the air's not saturated enough to rain."

"But if there's sufficient moisture . . ." Tuli started.

"It never gets 'sufficient,' Oriental chemist. Not when the dew points are as low as they are now. This Canadian air coming down the eastern slope of the ridge dries out whatever moisture we get. Sure, the water vapor's still there, but the relative humidity is way down. You get minor droplets, only about five or ten microns big. They're too light to fall! Need fifty-micron drops to get rain."

Walking toward the map, Tuli argued, "Then why not seed the clouds and force rainfall? If the moisture is available. . . ."

"Seeding's not the answer, unless you want to seed all day long, every day. Soon as you stop seeding, it'll stop raining. Cost a few million bucks a day to get decent rainfall, buddy. Blasted drought's cheaper'n that!"

"Then what do we do?" I asked.

"Make the natural environment work for us, instead of trying to work against it."

"And how do you do that?"

He gestured toward the viewscreen. "We've got to move that high-pressure ridge back over the Atlantic, just offshore."

I must have blinked.

"It's very simple, really," Tuli said, nearly grinning. "We only need to manipulate the weather over half the world."

Ted took me to his desk and launched into a detailed explanation. It was long and complex and I hardly understood half of it. But it boiled down to the fact that the cloud cover over the Arctic Ocean had been far less than normal for the past several years. That, Ted firmly believed, was the trigger that started a chain reaction that led to the New England drought.

"And that's causing the drought? Sunny weather around the Arctic Circle?" I wondered aloud.

"Not by itself, but it's the biggest reason. *And* it's something we can change. Right, Oriental chemist?"

Tuli shrugged. "There are several halogen compounds that will react to sunlight at high altitudes to produce clouds . . . we might be able to cloud over a fair-sized area that way."

"And start the ball rolling away from the drought pattern, through the breakup, and into normal conditions."

"We haven't proven that yet," Tuli cautioned. "Our laboratory experiments are on too small a scale to show if the chain reaction will follow. . . ."

"Okay, okay." Ted waved him down. "The rough numbers look good, though. We set up the cloud cover at the right spots in the Arctic. We work on the High over the Appalachians at the same time . . . try to weaken it enough so it'll break up naturally and re-form over the ocean. Once we get things rolling the right way, the atmosphere'll snap back to its usual balance and the drought'll be busted."

"You make it sound easy," I said.

"Sure. Like building the first atomic bomb." He went on with an hour's worth of things he needed done, which included weather modifications over Canada and Greenland, as well as over the ocean. He outlined work that had to be done on land, sea, and in the air.

I was starting to stagger. "But we'll need the cooperation of the Navy, the Air Force, the Atomic Energy Commission, and the State Department, just for starting! And what about the Canadians and the Danes? Or the United Nations. . . ."

He laughed at me. "Those aren't technical problems, old buddy. I'm telling you what we need. How to get 'em done is your end of the stick."

"Thanks a lot. Anything else?"

I shouldn't have asked. It took the rest of the morning for him to finish telling me.

"Ted, this is going to cost hundreds of millions!"

"Baloney! We're only going to be operating long enough to shift the atmosphere back to its normal balance. Then we leave it alone. Three months ought to do it, maybe less. And the cost'll be peanuts compared to what the drought's costing."

"And you really can do it?"

Tuli answered, "It will be slightly more difficult than our optimistic leader thinks, but he's essentially right. It can be done."

Ted grinned. "Thanks for the vote of confidence."

I was just beginning to realize, emotionally, what they had said. Talking about weather control and drought alleviation is one thing, but to see it actually begin to take shape, to see plans being laid for moving rainfall from one place to another. . . .

I walked back from Ted's desk to the mammoth viewscreen, fascinated by its swirling arrows and symbols.

"Ted . . . this . . . this is marvelous!"

"Does kind of shake you," he agreed. "Makes me feel like that character that first climbed Everest."

"Huh? Oh, you mean Hillary."

"Or Tenzing Norka," Tuli said.

"Tenzing, that's the one. The Sherpa." Ted sat on the desk, his eyes narrowing as if he were trying to picture the scene. "He was born right there, under the mountain. Spent all his life looking at it. Nobody had ever made it to the top. But he did. Some kick."

Tuli's round face was solemn. "Someday we may feel the same way."

"Someday soon," Ted added. "Nobody's ever been able to change the weather. But we're going to, friends. Sure as it rains on picnics, we're going to. So let's get to work!"

And we did. We all pitched into the job with an eagerness I'd never seen before. It was as if we had been hunting a crafty wild animal, on its trail for ages, and now we were closing in for the kill. Excitement crackled through the Lab. Ted and Tuli started working out the exact details of the modification missions they'd have to conduct: the chemicals to use, the amounts, the planes needed, the days they would operate, the effects they would have. My administrative staff began working on getting the men and materials we would need.

But beneath it all, I had the sickening feeling that it would never happen. I dreamed a lot of Rossman; wherever we turned, it seemed in my nightmares, Rossman would be blocking us, standing between us and our goal.

And the nightmare started to come true.

We had been conducting seeding experiments out over the open ocean for months, working on a month-to-month license granted by ESSA. Without it, we were prohibited from doing any seeding. Our application for the month of September was returned.

Refused.

It was a routine request, exactly the same as those we had put through since early in the spring. But ESSA rejected it. I took the tube train down to Washington the next morning.

It was brutally hot in the capital: even the air-conditioned taxis were muggy and sweltering. The trees were brown from lack of water and the sidewalks shimmered in the late August heat.

Everyone in ESSA, it seemed, was out of town. Everyone I asked to see, that is. A taxi hop across the blistering city brought me to the Pentagon. At least the military people had the courtesy to talk to me. But the Navy people flatly refused to cooperate with Aeolus' modification work, and the Air Force officers said they could work with the Weather Bureau, but not with a private firm—unless we had Government approval for our drought-breaking operation.

I was shut out. I even had trouble finding Jim Dennis. Finally, I tracked him down in the Capitol Building: he was in a committee session, but came right out when he got my note.

"I hope I didn't take you away from anything important."

"No," he said, grinning. "They're talking about appropriations. We'll go around the mulberry bush a few times before any real work gets done."

We paced down the ornate hallway outside the committee room, and I told him about my shutout at ESSA and the Pentagon.

He shook his head. Looking out a window at the wilting city, he murmured, "They've been talking about putting a dome over the District, like the Manhattan Dome. We could use city-wide air conditioning on a day like today." He turned to me. "What do you think Ted would say about that?"

I shrugged. "I think he'd rather put a dome on Rossman ... or whoever's slamming the door in our faces."

"It's Rossman, all right," Dennis said. "The word is out. He's got his own drought-control ideas. He's keeping it very, very quiet right now, but I've been able to learn that he plans to start some limited experiments next spring. In the meantime, he's going to do everything he can to keep you out of the picture."

"But ... it's not fair. It's not right!"

"I agree with you," the Congressman said. "But what good does that do? Rossman is known and respected in the Weather Bureau. He's got the power."

"Well, can't you do something?"

"If I were chairman of the Science Committee, maybe I could kick up a fuss. But I'm only a Congressman ... and a pretty new one, at that."

"There ought to be something we can do!" My mind

was racing, trying to figure a way. "How about arranging a meeting between Ted and Rossman? We can at least make him know we're on to his game. *And* that we might complain to the Science Committee."

He mulled it over for a moment. "I don't know if it will help any. But I'll do it. I'd like to see the two of them in the same room," he added, with a grin.

Ted literally exploded when I told him that evening about my day in Washington. Tuli, Barney, and I had to talk with him for hours. He was all for racing straight to the newspapers and screaming his head off. Finally I explained that Dennis was going to get Rossman to sit down with us and talk the whole thing over.

He nodded. He didn't speak, but merely nodded. I noticed his hands were clenching into fists, over and over again, like a gladiator testing his weapons in the final few moments of waiting before entering the arena.

The meeting took place in Congressman Dennis' office in Lynn. It was a pleasant enough spot, in a small office building that housed lawyers and insurance agents. Both sides had agreed to it as neutral territory.

We sat around Jim's desk, Dr. Rossman on one side and Ted and me on the other.

"I asked for this meeting," the Congressman said from his leather desk chair, "because Jerry here feels that Aeolus Research is being stymied by the Weather Bureau in its attempts to break the drought. Since the subject is probably the most important one in New England at the moment, I think it deserves our careful attention."

Ted and Dr. Rossman just glared at each other, so I said, "Aeolus is ready to start modification work in a week or two. If we're allowed to go ahead, we think we can break the drought this year. If not, it'll be another year —probably not 'til next autumn—before we have another chance to improve the situation."

"That may be," Rossman replied somberly. He had a paper clip from Jim's desk in his hands and was twisting it incessantly. "We've been studying several approaches to modifying the drought condition at the Climatology Division. We expect to spend this fall and winter doing laboratory experiments. Some small modification missions might be run in the spring, if everything goes well."

Ted couldn't stay silent any longer. "Won't work," he said flatly. "Need the fall and winter precipitation. Otherwise the water table'll never get high enough. Soon as the growing season begins you'll be back where you started. Worse."

"That's only your guess," Rossman snapped.

"No guess! You need the autumn rains and a winter's worth of snow and runoff, otherwise the spring storms are only a trickle. You'd get wetter in a bathtub."

"This autumn will be much too early to start full-scale modification work."

"For you, maybe. You're six months behind us. You'll do a little tinkering in the spring, give it up when it doesn't help enough, and then claim weather control's a waste of time and money. We're ready to go now. And we'll do the job *right!* All we need is permission."

The paper clip broke in Rossman's hands. "You can't fly out and try weather experiments just because you want to be first. Suppose the experiment doesn't work? Suppose something was missing from the calculations? Suppose a modification boomerangs and makes conditions worse instead of better?"

"Suppose there's an earthquake?" Ted mimicked, "or the sky starts falling in?"

"Let's not. . . ."

"Listen," Ted said. "We're not playing games. We've checked out the whole scheme. We've built theoretical models. We've done computer simulations. We've checked, point for point, exactly what'll happen every step of the way. Ask the MIT people; they know what we've done. We're ready to go now, and a year from now we couldn't be more ready. I can tell you exactly what the weather will be over New England, day by day, for the next two months. And I can tell what it'll be either way—with the modifications or without."

"You haven't convinced me or any other reputable meteorologist that your scheme will work."

"You don't *want* to be convinced!"

Ted was almost out of his chair. I reached up and put a hand on his shoulder. "Dr. Rossman," I said, "perhaps it would help if you'd come down to Aeolus and let us show you what we're planning to do. Perhaps then you could. . . ."

Rossman shook his head. "I simply can't allow modification experiments to take place until I'm convinced that every possible safeguard has been taken to make certain the results won't be harmful."

Ted slumped back in his chair. "Meaning six more months of diddling and cross-checking the work that's already been done."

"If necessary, yes." Rossman turned to Jim Dennis. "Our

first responsibility is to serve the public: *we're* not in business to turn a quick profit."

"Serve the public," Ted muttered. "Serve 'em another year of drought."

Rossman got to his feet. "There's no point in carrying this argument any further. When you finally grow up, Marrett, maybe you'll learn that being fast doesn't always make you right."

Ted growled back, "Age doesn't make you any smarter; just slower."

Rossman slammed out of the office. Jim Dennis shrugged helplessly. "I'm inclined to be on your side. But he's got all the votes. The ones that count."

We were a sad, dispirited crew when we got back to Aeolus that afternoon. Tuli, after hearing the news, moped in his lab. Ted sat at his desk, feet propped up, staring vacantly at the viewscreen map with the drought pattern on it. I couldn't sit still. I prowled around the place, getting strange looks from the people who were still busily working without knowing yet that their work was going to be for nothing.

Barney showed up around five thirty. She had heard the news, I could tell from the look on her face as I met her in the hall.

"Welcome to the funeral," I said.

"I came as soon as I could get away. The whole Division is buzzing about it."

"I'll bet."

"Ted must be furious."

"I think he's in a state of shock."

"Where is he?"

"Come on," I said.

But he was no longer in his room. Nor in Tuli's lab; they were both gone.

"Let's try the roof," I suggested.

Sure enough, that's where they were, standing amid the jumble of Weather Bureau equipment that made up the observation station.

"Come to see the sun go down?" Ted asked us. "And the future with it?"

"Is it that bad?" Barney tried to force a smile.

"Yep."

"Isn't there anything we can do?"

He shook his head. "Look around, what do you see? A few thousand dollars' worth of equipment, all marked, 'Property of U.S. Government: Do Not Touch.' That's where we stand. Surrounded by tools we can use better than they can . . . but we can't touch."

"Water, water everywhere," I mumbled to myself.

"Rossman's got the keys and we're locked out," Ted said. "Worst of it is, he's not going to do the job right. By the time he works up enough guts to really grab the problem and fix it, the drought'll be over anyway."

"But there will be pressure on him to produce," I said. "The farmers, the newsmen, the state governments, and Congress . . ."

Ted waved a disgusted hand at me. "What pressure? You heard him today, the Official Voice of Science. He'll just tell 'em the same fairy story he told Dennis . . . he's protecting the public from harebrained schemes. Weather modification could make things worse instead of better. By the time he gets done talking, the newsmen'll be down on their knees thanking him for rescuing 'em from kooky kids and their wild ideas."

He turned away and looked out toward the harbor. From our perch on the rooftop, we could see pleasure boats criss-crossing the water. A jetliner screamed down the airport runway and hurled itself into the sky.

"Why?" Ted slammed his fist against the guard rail. "Why is he blocking it? He knows it'll work! Why is he pussyfooting?"

"Because he wants the credit for being first," Barney said, "but he doesn't want to take the risks. He's very cautious."

"The plowhorse that wanted to win the Kentucky Derby," Ted grumbled.

"He wants the glory very much," Barney said. "He's worked all his adult life in the Weather Bureau, and done some very good work, but he's never been in the spotlight."

"He'll never get the spotlight unless he moves faster than he's planning to," Ted answered. "By the time he's ready to do some real weather control, it'll be old enough to write up in the Encyclopaedia Britannica."

"He can't move faster until he's perfected his version of your long-range forecasts," Tuli said. "Until he does that, he must go slowly."

Ted looked up at the Mongol. "You're right, Tuli. He needs the. . . ." His voice trailed off, and he frowned with concentration.

Finally, Ted said, "Suppose I went to Rossman and offered to pool forces with him?"

"What?"

"Okay, I know it sounds kinky, but listen. He wants the

glory, but he needs the forecasts. We want to get the job done, but we need his permission. Let's get together on it!"

"He'd laugh in your face," I said.

"Would he? Would he pass up the chance to grab the glory . . . and have somebody to dump the blame on if things go wrong?"

"It's crazy," I said.

Tuli said, "If it were someone else, Dr. Rossman might be tempted to try it. But not with you, Ted."

"Do you realize what you're saying, Ted?" Barney asked, wide-eyed.

"Sure."

"Dr. Rossman would never let anyone outside the Climatology Division assist him. Even if he *wanted* to work with you, it would have to be under his control."

Ted shrugged. "Then I'll ask him to take me back into the Division."

"You'll *what?*" I screamed. "Quit the Lab? You can't! This outfit was built for you, you can't just pack up and leave. It's . . . it's . . . treason, that's what it would be!"

"You're making money out of the Lab," he answered. "You'll still have the long-range forecasts and a topnotch technical staff."

"But you can't just pull out!"

"You don't own me, friend."

"But don't you have any sense of responsibility? Or gratitude? Or anything?"

His jaw settled ominously. "Listen. I don't have a few million bucks to play with, or an ancestral manor, or a dozen different businesses to dabble in. All I've got is weather control. We started this Lab to make weather control work. If I've got to leave the Lab to get weather control, I'll leave it. If I have to walk off the edge of this roof to get weather control, I'll do that too! Don't talk about responsibility or gratitude, buddy. I've made this Lab a money-making proposition. I've pulled your old man's dredges out of trouble. Now count your money and let me do the work I have to do."

He stormed past me and went downstairs, leaving me trembling with helpless fury.

I didn't see Ted again for a week. And when I did, it was only for a brief phone call one evening at my hotel room.

"Rossman gave in. I'm starting at Climatology tomorrow morning. I'm here at the Lab to pick up my junk . . . be here an hour or so, if you want to talk to me."

I punched the phone's "off" switch so hard it jammed shut.

From most points of view, Aeolus seemed almost unchanged. Tuli left with Ted, of course. He was very apologetic about it, in his Oriental way. But he went. So did a few other technical people.

I sat in the office and brooded while the staff ran things. The long-range forecasts were going smoothly and our work on drought control was being written into a series of reports for our customers. The only work that stopped was the preparations for the actual drought modifications.

I stayed at Aeolus for nearly a month. Barney called once or twice, but it was always very brief. Too busy working on the drought modifications, she said.

Two weeks after Ted left, we had a sharp thunderstorm that dropped nearly two inches of rain into the vanishing reservoirs. A few days later it drizzled for nearly thirty-six hours straight. Nothing spectacular, but everyone was grateful for it. Finally one morning late in September it clouded over and really poured rain, steadily, all day. Children ran home from school through puddles, splashing and sloshing in their yellow slickers and boots. People gathered at office windows to watch it, grinning. Grown men and women dug out old umbrellas and overshoes and actually went for walks in the first prolonged rain of the year.

I couldn't stand it any more. I bolted out of the office, drove through the rainy streets to the hotel, and started packing. I was finished with Ted and Barney and the whole idea of weather control. I was going back to Hawaii.

12. *Shifting Winds*

I THREW things blindly into my travel bag while the rain streamed down the window of my room. Clothes, shoes, shaving gear, everything stuffed in as fast as I could pull it from drawers and shelves.

The door buzzer sounded. "It's open!" I yelled.

Barney stepped in. "Jerry, isn't it wonderful! The rain. . . ."

She stopped when she saw what I was doing. She stood by the doorway in a dripping raincape and pushed a lock of glistening hair back away from her face.

"You're leaving?"

"Yes," I said, still packing.

"Because of Ted."

"Right again."

I walked into the bathroom to check the medicine cabinet. Everything was cleared out.

"When are you going?"

"On the first flyable machine that's heading for Hawaii."

Barney let the cape slip off her shoulders and drop on the chair by the door.

"I suppose I don't blame you," she said.

"That's generous."

"Jerry, don't be sarcastic."

"Why not? I thought you like guys who are sarcastic, and tough, and throw temper tantrums."

"I don't like people who run away."

I slammed the travel bag shut. "What do you expect me to do? Sit at my desk and count money while you and Ted soar on to new heights of scientific marvels? What's left for me to do around here? Nothing. Ted's got what he wants and you've got what you want. So I'll go back home and try to forget the whole mess."

"What do you mean, I've got what I want?"

"Ted's back with you, isn't he? You're together every day now; working side by side for sweet science. Just the two of you, with your Asiatic sidekick. The little rich boy from the islands has outlived his usefulness."

"Is that what you think?"

"I saved his neck when he was ready to throw in the towel. Now he doesn't need me any more. And as long as he's with you, you don't need me any more either. So why should I hang around? Just to watch his rain fall?"

"If that's true, Jerry," she said, "then why did I come here?"

I didn't have an answer for that one.

"If you can talk quietly for a few minutes," she said, going to the sofa, "perhaps I can show you how wrong you are."

"*I'm* wrong?"

"Ted's an unforgivable lout," she said, "there's no argument about that. The way he treated you was shameful. But if you'll listen to me for a minute, I think you'll see why he's the way he is."

"I don't want any amateur psychoanalysis of the young genius," I snapped.

"No, you'd rather run away home and hide behind your father!"

Her voice was suddenly sharp with real anger; I had never seen her angry before.

"Ted treated you horribly, there's no excuse for it. I expected you to be hurt and mad at him. But I didn't think you'd be so sorry for yourself."

"All right," I said. "Just why did you come?"

"Because Ted owes you an apology, but he'll never make it himself. So I thought I should."

"As his chosen representative?"

"You're being sarcastic again," she said.

I went over and sat beside her.

Barney said, "Ted operates in a world of his own. I've spent hours shouting at him about the way he treated you, but it makes no impression on him. He couldn't apologize even if he wanted to; he's much too stubborn for it. And besides, he's convinced that he's done the best thing. . . ."

"The best thing?"

"He wants to stop the drought. Going back to Climatology was the only way to do it. Do you think he enjoyed it? Have you any idea of what it took for him to ask Dr. Rossman to take him back again? To offer to take all the responsibility if the experiments fail, but stay out of the limelight if they work? I couldn't do that; none of us could. But Ted did. Without flinching."

"He's a madman," I muttered.

"He's breaking the drought, no matter who gets the

eventual credit for it. And he's certain that he did the right thing. He thinks that if you're angry, it's because you're stubborn and shortsighted."

"That's a very convenient way to look at it."

"It's not rationalization, Jerry. He really believes it. Nothing's more important to Ted than getting the job done—and done right. Anything that stands in his way . . . he has no patience for."

I looked past Barney's face to the dripping window. "I guess he's got the job done, all right."

She seemed to relax a little. "I wanted to come see you sooner, but we've been literally locked in the building for the past week and a half. It's been an impossible time. You know what a slave driver he is."

I had to smile. "You do look tired."

She nodded.

"Would you like some dinner?"

"Yes, that would be fine."

"I'll have it sent up."

I punched out a selection on the menu dial and within a few minutes the dinner was sliding out of the wall receptacle and onto the table. I rolled the table to the sofa.

"Are you still going to leave?" Barney asked as we ate.

"I don't know," I said.

"I wish you wouldn't."

And I wish you meant that, I said to myself.

After we finished, and I was fitting the dinner tray back into the wall receptacle, she asked again:

"Jerry, are you going to leave or stick it out?"

I watched the tray slide into the wall slot, taking the dishes with it.

"Does it make any difference?" I asked.

"Certainly it does."

"Why?"

"We need you, Jerry. Ted needs you; he needs all of us, all the people he can trust. Now more than ever."

"It's for Ted, then."

"And for me too, Jerry. I don't want you to leave. I told you that."

"Yes, I know you told me."

She stepped closer to me. "I mean it Jerry. Please don't leave."

I pulled her to me and kissed her. We held each other for a moment and then, very gently, she moved away.

"Jerry, it used to be that I wasn't sure of anything except Ted. Now I'm not even sure about that any more."

I had to smile. "That's the trouble with being a mere mortal. Now if we were supermen, like you-know-who, we'd never have any doubts about anything."

"Don't be so sure," she said seriously. "I know Ted takes people for granted and rides roughshod over anything in his way . . . but he has his doubts; about himself, about the work he wants to do. Just because he doesn't let anyone see them doesn't mean they don't exist."

"I guess you're right. He puts up a darned good front, though."

Barney turned toward the door. "Where'd I leave my raincape? It's time for me to go. . . ."

"I'll drive you home."

"No, that's all right. The rain's let up now, and it's not far on the slideway."

"Will I see you tomorrow?" I asked as I helped her into the cape.

"You're staying?"

"For a while, at least."

"Why don't you come over to Climatology for lunch? I think you and Ted should shake hands."

"And come out fighting?"

"What?"

"It's an old prizefighting expression."

She laughed. "See, you're telling jokes."

"Maybe I'm being sarcastic again."

"No, not any more."

I walked her down the hall to the elevator, saw her off, then ran back to my room, opened the jam-packed suitcase, and sprinkled its contents all over the floor.

Twenty-three thousand miles above the mouth of the Amazon River, the meteorologists aboard the Atlantic Station synchronous satellite watched a circular band of clouds building up in the mid-Atlantic. They televised their photographs to the National Hurricane Research Center in Miami, and within an hour patrol planes took off for the young storm. By the time they reached it, the hurricane had developed an eye and wind speeds of more than ninety knots. An inch of rain per hour was being poured over a six-thousand-square-mile area of the ocean. And the storm was moving westward. How far would it go? Where would it strike? No one knew. Warnings went out across the entire eastern seaboard, the Gulf Coast, and through the islands of the Caribbean. Hurricane alert. A thousand megatons of energy was on the loose and heading toward the fragile realm of men.

The morning was cloudy, and by the time I had 'coptered out to Climatology for lunch, it was starting to rain again.

Barney met me in the lobby. "Ted's group is in a new set of offices," she said, "over in the annex building."

She guided me through corridors and a covered walkway that connected the main building with the annex. Rain drummed hard on the low metal roof of the walkway, as we crossed it. The annex itself had that temporary, prefabricated look about it. There was no real ceiling, just the exposed underside of the roof, with all the structural braces and pipes and airshafts showing. Most of the building was filled with clanging, chatter-filled machine shops. The "offices" were made up of five-foot-high partitions, jury-rigged together to form enclosures.

"It's a little damp in here when it rains," Barney said over the machine-shop noise, "and it can get pretty hot when the weather's warm."

I followed her through the cramped makeshift corridors. You could see over the partitions right into the cubbyhole offices.

"Ted's place is down there," she said, pointing.

"You actually work in here?"

"I don't . . . I'm still in computing, where all we have to contend with is the hum of the machines and refugees from the annex who come over to see what real air conditioning feels like."

"This is terrible!"

We reached the end of the corridor and stepped into a corner room made up of two partitions and two of the walls of the annex building itself. Ted wasn't there, but you could see his stamp: drawing table piled high with charts, viewscreen map on the farther wall, cluttered desk, and the inevitable row of coffeepots.

"Welcome to Shangri-la!"

We turned and saw Ted hurrying down the corridor toward us. He was carrying a portable TV set.

"Come on, pull up a chair," he said, brushing past us to put the TV on his desk. "Glad you came, Jerry."

"I can see that you've been living in the lap of luxury since you left Aeolus," I said, going to one of the chairs.

Barney sat next to me. "Tuli calls this area Shangri-la."

"Rossman could have found you better quarters," I said.

Ted shrugged. "It's a dump all right. Part of the price we had to pay. I came to him, remember, he didn't come to me."

"I know."

"In a way, this lousy environment helps," he said cheerfully. "Everybody's got that basic-training spirit—you know, 'we're all in this together and we've got to help each other if we want to survive.' So the work gets done."

"That's the important thing," Barney said.

"Speaking of Rossman," Ted went on, "he's going to be on TV in a minute. Special show out of Washington. About the drought."

He flicked the TV set on. After four or five commercials, the show started. Dr. Rossman was flanked by the President's Science Adviser, Dr. Jerrold Weis, and by the Director of the Environmental Science Services Administration, a retired admiral named Correlli.

Tuli drifted into the office as the commentator was making introductory remarks. He nodded a grave hello to me and went behind the desk to stand beside Ted.

Dr. Weis made some general remarks about bringing together the scientific capabilities of the nation, and Admiral

Correlli spoke briefly about how wonderful ESSA was. Then came Dr. Rossman's turn. The camera closed in on his long, somber face as he began talking about the conditions that had caused the drought. He spoke slowly, carefully, the way a man does when he's not sure he's being understood. Gradually I began to realize that he was telling the same story—using the same words, almost—that Ted did that night so many weeks earlier when he first explained the drought problem to us.

The TV camera cut to a map. It was one of those that Ted had shown at the July Fourth conference.

"That's your work!" I blurted.

Ted smiled grimly. "Just the first slide . . . there's more."

Rossman kept talking and showing Ted's slides. I watched the drought condition change just as Ted said it would: the high-pressure cell moved off beyond the coast and the rain-giving southerly airflows came up over the eastern seaboard again. The TV screen showed films of planes flying seeding missions, and nuclear submarines being checked by engineers wearing protective antiradiation suits.

"They look like men from Mars," the TV commentator said, with a measured amount of awe in his voice.

"Yes, they do," Dr. Rossman answered.

The camera cut back to the four men in the studio.

"Well, the rainfall we've been getting certainly is concrete evidence that your work is a success," the commentator said heartily.

"Thank you," Dr. Rossman allowed himself a modest smile. "I think we've shown that weather modification can be employed to help ease critical weather problems . . . if the work is done under careful control, with all the proper safeguards."

I glanced at Ted. He was struggling to stay calm. He had taken a pencil in one big hand and was flexing it between his fingers.

"So it's now safe to say that the drought is a thing of the past," the commentator chirped.

Rossman nodded. "My group's two-month forecast indicates that precipitation levels should be slightly above normal for the entire area east of the Appalachians. Of course, my forecasts aren't foolproof, but they're good evidence that we're on the way out of the drought."

"*His* forecasts," Barney whispered.

"And now," the commentator said, "I believe that Dr. Weis has an announcement to make."

The camera switched to the President's Science Adviser. He had a pleasant, squarish face, so creased and tanned that he looked more like a cowboy than a physicist.

"As a result of Dr. Rossman's pioneering work on weather modification, exemplified by his alleviation of the serious drought that had affected the northeast sector of the nation, I have recommended to the President that he be considered for the National Medal of Science."

Snap! Ted broke the pencil.

"As you know, the National Medal of Science is awarded each year to. . . ."

Ted flicked the set off savagely.

"The National Medal," Barney said, shocked. "It's not fair. He doesn't deserve it."

"I suspect," Tuli said, "that Dr. Rossman is just as surprised about the award as we are."

"He can't accept it," I said. "The whole story will come out into the open."

Ted looked at the shattered pieces of the pencil in his hand, and dropped them into his wastebasket. "The story won't circulate very far. What'd you say if Albert Einstein's housekeeper popped up and claimed she figured out the laws of relativity and her boss took the credit?"

"That's not the same thing at all. . . ."

"Is for now, friend. Important thing is that the drought's broken, and weather mods are respectable now. That's a big jump in the right direction. Rossman knows the score, and so does the Chief, and your Congressman friend. Okay, Rossman gets the credit for this one. In public. We've got the talent."

I shook my head. "There's a fifty-thousand-dollar prize attached to that award, isn't there?"

"Peanuts," Ted snapped. "Money follows talent, pal. I'm young and willing to work. Which reminds me, I need you here. How about becoming a public servant?"

13. *Storm Clouds*

For an instant, I couldn't believe I had heard Ted correctly. "What did you say?"

"I want you to work here. We need you."

"You must be joking. . . ."

"No joke. Look around this dump." His arms swept around in an all-inclusive gesture. "Think Rossman *likes* having us here? Think he's going to feel comfy with that National Science Medal around his neck as long as we're here to stare him down? There's going to be trouble around here sooner or later, and I need all the friends I've got."

"What makes you think I'm friendly?" I heard myself ask.

Ted sat up sharply. "You're not still sore about me leaving Aeolus? Only thing I could do, Jerry. You know that."

"And now you want me to walk out on Aeolus too."

He made a helpless shrug. "We're getting buried in paperwork, Rossman's piling it higher every day. Trying to drown us in red tape. We go too fast for him; he was scared to death about the drought mods, now he's worried about what we'll spring on him next. So he's trying to slow us down with paperwork. You can help us get out from under. . . ."

I couldn't sit still any more. Getting up from my chair, I glanced at Barney. She was watching me, but I couldn't tell from her expression what she wanted me to do.

"Ted, if you had been with Santa Anna's army at the Alamo, you'd have had the nerve to ask Davy Crockett to change sides!"

"What sides? We all want the same thing . . . weather control. I need your help."

"Then you can *buy* my help. From Aeolus Research Laboratory!"

He blinked. "Now wait a minute. . . ."

"No, you wait," I said, standing in front of his desk. "There are eighty people at Aeolus who earn their living from the contracts the Laboratory gets. You walked out and took with you the best chances we had of getting really big contracts for weather-modification work. Okay. But those eighty people can still do good work. They can help you with paperwork, with computations, with long-range forecasts, and lots of other things. They can give you far more help than I can alone, no matter which roof I sit under. And if you think I'm going to walk out on them the way you did, just because you want another paper-shuffler to talk to, then think again! You know a lot more about the weather than you do about people."

Ted leaned back in his chair, frowning silently. Then a grin spread over his rugged face. "You can be a real ball of fire when you want to be, Jerry. What's more, you're right . . . Aeolus can help us out. Help us a lot, come to think of it."

I almost fell over. Barney looked at me as if to say, *Good going.*

Tuli said, "But how can you get Dr. Rossman to agree to spending the money for hiring Aeolus to help us?"

"I think," Ted answered, "that with that nice, shiny National Medal in his pocket, he sort of owes us a favor. I'll talk to him about it as soon as he gets back from Washington." Turning back to me, he asked, "You're not too sore to work with us if we sign a contract for Aeolus and pay you, are you?"

"I'm not interested in the doggone money, Ted, you know that. I just won't run out on the people at Aeolus."

"Okay, simmer down. You made your point, and it's a good one. Should've thought of it myself."

"Then we'll all be working together again." Barney looked pleased about it.

Ted stuck his hand out across the desk. "Welcome back to the team, buddy."

I reached out and shook hands with him, but for the first time since I had met Ted, I wasn't really happy about working with him.

Meteorologists dubbed the hurricane Lydia, since it was the twelfth tropical storm or hurricane to threaten populated areas. She traveled westward from her mid-ocean spawning place, following the trade winds toward the West Indies. Then, after three days, she turned suddenly and aimed toward the Florida coast. Disaster warnings flashed along the peninsula. Lydia's central wind speed was almost a hundred knots, her rains devastating. Across the Bahamas she struck, flattening palms, smashing seawalls with titanic waves, piling boats and piers alike against the rocks, blowing off roofs, snapping power lines, flooding roads and homes and towns, destroying, terrorizing, killing. When the island skies cleared again, dazed and weary men surveyed the field of a battle they had lost. Thousands were homeless. Towns were without electricity or drinking water. The survivors were battered, hungry, injured. Planes brought in medical supplies and food while Lydia gathered strength, poised just off the Florida coast near Miami.

The day following my visit to Ted's new quarters at Climatology, Barney called me at Aeolus and invited herself to lunch. We met at one of the Back Bay towers' roof-top restaurants.

It was a warm, sunny day—unusually nice for the beginning of November. From our table by the window we could see the distant hills that marked the location of the Climatology building. Barney sat next to the window, her yellow hair catching the sunlight and framed by the clear, deep blue of the sky.

"Ted talked with Dr. Rossman first thing this morning," she said after we ordered the meal. "You should be getting a contract for Aeolus to help us with the long-range forecasts and some of the administrative chores."

I nodded.

"You really startled Ted yesterday," she went on, "when you told him off. He never expected you to shout him down."

"I wasn't telling anybody off. It just made me sore to think that he'd expect me to jump from Aeolus the way he did. He asked me to turn my back on the people I'm responsible for . . . just as if he were asking you to pass the salt."

Barney inadvertently started to reach for the saltshaker, then caught herself. We both laughed.

"See, he's got us both trained," I said.

"He needs us, Jerry," she said, her smile dimming. Earnestly, she added, "Don't be angry with him. Please, Jerry, no matter how hard it is, please don't be angry with him. Try to remember that he needs every friend he has."

"Then why does he trample on people?"

She shook her head. "It's the way he is. We'll have to accept him that way. He won't change."

I knew she was right about Ted. And I knew I could never argue with her, whether she was right or wrong. "Okay, we'll accept him the way he is. But we don't have to like it. He's a fanatic, and fanatics can be dangerous."

"Yes, I know," she agreed. "But they're just as dangerous to themselves as to anyone else."

Miami took the brunt of the hurricane. The plush Miami Beach hotels were dark and empty as the invading seas and wind tore through them, smashing windows and flooding ground floors with a massive storm tide. Luxury automobiles were swept by the surging waves completely off the island, most of them to disappear forever into the sea. The city of Miami was devastated, its waterfront wrecked, its civil defense shelters jammed with fleeing thousands. Planes were ripped from their moorings at airfields and lofted wildly, to crash and pinwheel against the drenched ground. People huddled for hours in homes and buildings, without radio reception, without phones, with nothing to listen to but their own frightened voices and the howling fury outside that was breaking windows, toppling poles, tearing down signs, and seemingly trying to erase mankind from the landscape. Finally, Lydia turned up the peninsula, spreading death and havoc wherever she touched.

Lydia was still a big topic of discussion at Climatology the following week, when I visited Ted's shop. My official reason for going there was to take care of some of the paperwork that would lead to a contract between the Division and Aeolus. I spent the morning filling out forms, and by noontime I was hungry enough even for the cafeteria's brand of food. But Ted and Barney took me out to a little pizza place in the next town.

It was starting to rain again as we pulled into the restaurant's parking lot.

"Secondary storm," Ted mused. "Spin-off from Lydia."

"She was some hurricane," I said as we scampered from the car to the restaurant door. "Miami's been wrecked; damage estimates are in the billion-dollar range."

"It's a shame we didn't have long-range forecasts to predict where the storm would strike," Barney said.

By now we were inside. We picked a booth and ordered pizza.

"Would a long-range forecast have been able to help Miami very much?" I wondered aloud.

Shrugging, Ted answered, "Be tough to pinpoint exactly where and when the storm'll hit. Too many variables. Hurricanes are tricky—very sensitive, even with all that size and power."

"But a longer warning time would have helped the people to get ready for the storm," Barney suggested.

"Not interested in warnings," Ted grumbled. "I want to stop those storms. Nothing worse than knowing where it's going to hit but not being able to do a blasted thing about it."

I looked out the restaurant window at the rain. "Looks like a northeaster blowing up."

That made him grin. "Sound like a real Yankee there. But you're right. We're in for heavy weather."

After the pizza arrived and we were halfway through, Barney asked, "Just what does Dr. Rossman intend to do now that the drought's finished?"

Ted made a sour face. "Tell you what he's *not* going to do: weather control. He wants us to check and recheck everything about the drought, for the whole northern hemisphere, for the next six months. Says he wants to make certain we didn't cause any harm. Just another one of his delaying tactics."

While I was struggling with a taffy-like slab of cheese atop a pizza slice, Ted went on, "He's dead-set against another modification job; scared to death of anything new."

Here we go again, I thought.

"Just to keep me quiet, though," Ted went on, "he's given in on the long-range forecasts. He's letting us send them out to the Weather Bureau networks on an experimental basis. The forecasts won't be made public, but the offices around the country'll start comparing 'em with what really happens. That's why we need Aeolus, old Yankee buddy. Have to start cranking out forecasts for the whole continental U.S."

"That's a big order," I mumbled, from behind the pizza.

"Too big for Climatology to handle, unless Rossman gets permission to double his staff. Which he won't try for. Lot easier to cut a contract than fire a hundred or so Government employees."

"Thanks for the encouragement."

He laughed. "Listen. We've got to figure out a way to get him to agree to more weather-control work. Without getting *me* fired again!"

"That would look bad on your employment record," I couldn't help saying.

Barney stepped in before Ted could reply. "Just what are you thinking of, Ted?"

"Not sure, yet. But we've got to do something that'll force Rossman to take the next step. Otherwise he'll just sit where he is, safe and respected, and admire his Medal."

"Any ideas?" I asked.

"Couple," he said, looking out at the thickening rain.

"Been hearing some rumbles from friends in New York that the Manhattan Dome's got some air-pollution troubles. Maybe you can look into that, Jerry. Rossman'd bounce off the ceiling if he knew I was getting into it.

"And there's an Air Force major coming to see me this afternoon, to talk about weather control and military problems. Might be the kind of road we can take to get a *real* project going."

"I never thought about the military uses of weather control," I said.

"Something to think about. Why don't you stick around this afternoon. This might be fun."

So I went back to Climatology with them. Ted's office was clammy, and you could hear the rain drumming hard against the metal roof. He turned on an electric heater near his desk and then poured coffee for me and himself. Barney had gone back to the computations section.

Major Vincent arrived halfway through the coffee. He

was chunky, not too tall, and almost completely bald. But his roundish face was young-looking, nearly babyish.

"I'm with the Foreign Technology Division," the major said after Ted had sat him down and handed him a cup of coffee. "Our main job is to keep the Air Force informed as to what other nations are doing in various technological fields."

"Such as weather control?" Ted asked, sitting behind his desk.

"Well, maybe. Right now FTD is officially interested in how well other nations can predict the weather, and perhaps make small-scale modifications . . . like clearing fog around an airfield, that sort of thing."

"But you're worrying about whether the Reds can tamper with our weather. . . . At least, you should be."

The major shifted his weight uncomfortably in his chair. "I am worried about that, you bet I am. And not just about the Reds, either. Any nation that can control weather has a weapon as powerful as ICBM's."

Ted got up and went down to the chalkboard behind his desk. "Jerry's heard this lecture before . . . it's sort of my standard speech about what you need for weather control."

And he launched into his routine about turbulence theory, long-range forecasts, energy sources, and such. As he spoke, Major Vincent took a small notebook from his tunic and began writing in shorthand.

When Ted finished, the major snapped the notebook shut. Ted had filled the chalkboard with words, diagrams, and equations.

"This is what we need," the major said. "If we know

what to look for, we can tell what's going on in other countries."

"Without calling in the spies," Ted added.

"FTD isn't in the espionage business."

"Not in public," Ted jabbed.

The major decided to change the subject. "Now take this hurricane that just hit Florida. . . ."

"Lydia."

"Yes. Now, couldn't that have been formed artificially? Or maybe deliberately steered to hit the United States?"

Ted shrugged elaborately. "It's possible. We don't know how to do it yet, but another country might be ahead of us."

Shaking his head, the major said, "The more I think about it, the more important it sounds to me. Suppose this drought you people broke up was the work of an enemy power? Why, with weather control you could bring a country to its knees without its ever knowing it had been attacked!"

"Never thought of it that way," Ted answered.

"Suppose an enemy could control our weather," the major mused, going to the chalkboard. "Every time it rains, I get nervous."

"I really don't think anyone's far enough advanced yet to do it," I said.

"Maybe not." The major erased Ted's work from the board. Then he stepped back and squinted at the faint smudged images still visible. He took a piece of chalk and scribbled heavily over them, then erased the whole board again.

"There," he said. "It's clean. That's a little habit you get into when you deal with classified information."

"There's nothing classified about it," Ted said.

"Maybe it ought to be."

Frowning, Ted said, "You can't classify the weather."

"No, I guess not. But weather *control* is something else again."

I didn't realize how seriously the major meant those words until a couple of weeks later when Aeolus was invaded by a squad of Government Security inspectors. Their job, as the head man explained to me, was to make certain that the Laboratory was physically safe for holding documents that might be classified Secret.

"But we're not doing any classified work," I protested.

"We've got a request here from the Air Force," he said, brandishing an official-looking yellow sheet, "to check out Aeolus Research Laboratory for a Secret facility clearance. All your people will be getting personal Security checks, too."

"What does that mean?"

"It means that if you've hired any people who can't be cleared for handling Secret work, they'll have to be moved to a separate building or fired altogether."

"But we're not doing Secret work!"

He waved the yellow sheet again. "According to the Air Force, you will be."

The inspectors poked everywhere, setting up locations for guard desks, slapping padlocks on file cabinets, ordering us to get special wastebins for discarding classified material, and explaining to my one-girl library staff how to stamp, store, distribute, and keep records of classified documents.

In the middle of the uproar, I phoned Ted.

"Was just going to call you," he said. "Got the Security people on your back?"

"All over the place."

He grinned. "They locked Rossman's desk on him while he was at lunch. Took him an hour to get a key for it. Turned him purple."

"Is all this fuss necessary?" I asked.

"Guess so, if we're going to work for the Air Force."

Just then Tuli—calm, stoic Tuli—came storming into the view of the phone screen, his fists clenched and his eyes blazing. Barney was right behind him, looking close to tears.

"What's going on?" Ted asked.

Wordlessly, Tuli handed him a slip of yellow paper. Ted scanned it, and his face twisted into an angry frown.

"Look at this!"

He held the memorandum up to the screen:

SINCE FOREIGN NATIONALS ARE BARRED FROM ACCESS TO CLASSIFIED INFORMATION, IT IS NECESSARY TO SUSPEND P. O. BARNEVELDT AND T. R. NOYON INDEFINITELY, PENDING FULL SECURITY INVESTIGATION.

14. Bitter Winter

I STARED at the yellow memo, trying to think of what to do first.

"Let me call Major Vincent," I said. "I wanted to talk to him about what's been happening here at Aeolus anyway."

"I'll call him," Ted said, tight-lipped.

"No, you'd better not." I knew that after three words to the major, Ted would be shouting. "I'll talk to him and call you back."

Getting the major on the phone wasn't easy. He had been transferred out of the Ohio base of the Foreign Technology Division and was now quartered in Washington.

"I've been moved to a special group," he said when I finally tracked him down. "We're setting up a weather-control project. Marrett's outfit and yours will both be able to help us on it."

I explained about the security uproar both at Climatology and Aeolus. Major Vincent looked sympathetic but helpless.

"I know you're not working on any classified stuff at your

Lab . . . yet. But we've got to be sure that you'll be okay to handle Secret material when the time comes. Which will be soon, believe me."

"But what about Ted's two closest aides being suspended?" I demanded. "That's going to ruin his work."

He looked truly unhappy. "I battled that out with the Security people here before the order was sent. Believe me, I fought them for a solid week. But they've got the rules and regulations on their side. I wish there was something I could do to help, but my hands are tied."

"Ted is going to go off like a five-stage rocket," I said. "He won't work for you unless——"

"He'll have to work for us," the major snapped. "Listen, I'm as easy to get along with as anybody, but this project isn't going to depend on any one man. If Marrett can't live with the Security regulations, we'll get somebody else to run his shop at Climatology and he'll be out."

"You mean there's absolutely nothing that can be done? These people haven't done anything wrong, and they'll be thrown out of their jobs. That's not fair!"

"Well, maybe I can swing a deal about the girl. She's taken out citizenship papers, from what the Security people tell me. And her native country is an ally of ours. But the other fellow is from Mongolia. They're no friends of ours."

"They're not enemies either," I answered.

Major Vincent put up his hands in an "I've-done-all-I-can-do" kind of gesture.

Ted was glowering angrily as I told him of the major's offer.

"So he'll let Barney hang on. What's wrong with Tuli? Air Force afraid he's part of the yellow peril?"

"I think it's the red menace they're afraid of. Mongolia is officially a socialist nation."

"Red menace, yellow peril . . . put 'em together and you get an orange mess." He was far from joking about it. "So what do we do, ship Tuli back to Mongolia in a crate?"

"If he's officially suspended," I said, "why can't he work temporarily for Aeolus? Just until this mess gets straightened out. We can set him up in a separate office close to our building."

Ted thought a moment. "Maybe that'll work. There's this air-pollution problem the Manhattan Dome people got themselves stuck with. Tuli could help 'em straighten it out. Can't do it as a Climatology employee, thanks to Rossman. But as an Aeolus man. . . ."

I nodded. "I'll get the paperwork started right away. Tuli can join our staff as a temporary consultant."

"Okay," Ted agreed. "But this whole military operation is wrong-end first. Been thinking about it. If they're going to handle weather control like a secret weapon, the whole idea's going to get bogged down in trouble."

The wind had come a long way. About three weeks earlier it had been a cold, dry blast scouring the Siberian tundra as the November freeze swept southward past Lake Baikal. It blew out onto the wide Pacific, whipping deep swells and drawing moisture from the sea. The west wind invaded America on an eight-hundred-mile-wide front, sending California farmers to their smudge pots to prevent a freeze on the last of the fruit harvest. As it climbed over the Rockies, the wind dropped first rain, then a foot-thick blanket of snow as it surrendered its captured moisture. It was a dry wind again when it slid down the other side of the mountains and across the southwestern desert. It curved out toward the Gulf Coast, picked up a little more water vapor and—guided by the jet stream—rushed northeastward into New England. By the time it reached Boston it had cooled down to its dew point and sprinkled a fine powdery snow over the area. Delighted children rushed to their cellars to find sleds. Grumbling adults went to their garages, muttering about snow tires and New England winters.

Jim Dennis called a few days before Thanksgiving and invited the four of us to his house for the holiday afternoon.

"I want you to meet someone," he said, "who's interested in your problems with the Pentagon's weather project."

Surprised, I said, "I didn't realize you knew about it. The project's supposed to be secret."

"You'd be surprised what a Congressman hears," he answered, with a sly smile.

I took Barney, Ted, and Tuli to Thornton for Thanksgiving dinner, and then we drove out to the Dennis house. It started to snow as we approached Lynn.

"Right on schedule," Ted said, looking at his wristwatch. "Should be a snowy winter this year."

The Dennis household was filled with children, friends, political aides, petitioning voters, and neighbors. Jim was shuttling back and forth between his office and the living room, which were separated by the house's main hallway. The living room was crowded with politically minded adults of one sort or another. Business problems. We fit into that category, but Mrs. Dennis took us in tow first, introduced us to everybody in the dining room, where a second shift of Thanksgiving dinner seemed to be getting started, and ushered us back into the kitchen.

She had charge of the children and the nonpolitical

adults. The dining room, kitchen, and all play areas were her domain. Somehow she managed to keep everyone happy and fed, and the children safely occupied, while still looking calmly unruffled. Barney watched her with unabashed awe.

"You can put your coats on the table next to the stove," she said, pointing to a magnificent old black woodburner. "Jim might be tied up for a while. Would you like some dinner? How about fruitcake and cider? Or pie?"

We all declined except Ted, who could always somehow stow another piece of pie. It might have been an awkward half hour as we stood in the kitchen with a gang of strangers and children, but Mrs. Dennis managed to make us feel at home. She knew us all by name, and soon had us talking about the weather—and what we could do about it.

Ted was just starting to hit his conversational stride when Jim walked in, shirtsleeves rolled up, tie loosened, grinning happily.

"Holidays are kind of confused around here sometimes," he said to us. "Sorry you couldn't come for dinner. I ate enough turkey to make up for it, though."

"We've been talking about the snow," Mrs. Dennis said. "Ted thinks it's going to stop in another hour or so."

Jim laughed. "Ted doesn't think. He knows."

"Hope so," Ted replied.

"Okay," the Congressman said, "so don't bother getting out the shovels and boots. Now, how about the four of you coming to the quiet end of the house. And Mary, could you bring us another pot of coffee?"

"That's the only time I see you during the holidays," she said, "when you're hungry or thirsty."

"Politics is a rough life."

The Congressman's office was small but surprisingly quiet.

"I soundproofed it myself," he said. "With five kids and all their friends around the house . . . it was soundproofing or insanity."

He gestured to the chairs. I picked a rocker. Three walls of the office were covered with bookshelves; the fourth had a pair of windows with several framed photographs between them.

After Mrs. Dennis delivered the coffee and we poured ourselves some, Jim began, "The Science Committee is going to start hearings in January about the Weather Bureau's work. Naturally, your weather-control idea will become big news."

"So that's it. . . ."

"Wait, there's more. The Pentagon has been pushing hard to get their project going. Their work will be secret, if and when they get the go-ahead from Congress and the White House. In the meantime, it's no secret that they're driving for a weather-control project. It's all over Washington, and it could become a political football, first class. Now if—"

The doorbell rang. Jim said, "I think that's our mystery guest."

He went out into the hall and greeted a man at the front door. "Glad you could come," we heard him say. "Here, leave your coat on the telephone table and come in. They're all here."

We recognized the man who stepped into the office as Dr. Jerrold Weis, the President's Science Adviser. He was small, slight, with a high nasal voice. He looked even more tanned in person than he did on TV. His handshake was strong and his gaze penetrating.

After the introductions, Dr. Weis wound up in my rocking chair. I found some leaning room on a windowsill.

"So you are the young geniuses," Dr. Weiss said, digging a pipe out of his jacket pocket, "who broke up the drought."

"And who want to control the weather," Jim Dennis said. "Tell him about it, Ted."

It took a couple of hours, and even some equation-writing on the Congressman's stationery to settle some of Dr. Weis' technical questions. Ted roamed the small room ceaselessly as he spoke, shaping ideas with his hands, going through the whole history of the long-range forecasts, Aeolus Research, the drought, and Major Vincent's project.

Dr. Weis puffed thoughtfully on his pipe as he listened.

"I believe one point is clear," the Science Adviser said when Ted finally slowed to a halt. "Unless we act to prevent it, there will be a classified military weather-control program underway within a year."

Ted nodded.

"And a classified military program," Dr. Weis went on, "will dominate the entire field of research. Congress won't want to support two or three different Government agencies all doing the same work. If the Pentagon gets a weather-control program going first, they'll force everyone else to work under their terms."

"Is that so terrible?" Barney asked.

Ted answered, "Already making trouble for you and Tuli. Once they really get started, the Security lid gets welded onto everything. The work'll be aimed at using the weather as a weapon. The push'll be to do things that show a big effect; research and everything else has to have a payoff that the top brass can see right away."

"It's not the proper way to do this kind of work," Dr. Weis agreed. "Weather control could be a powerful tool for peace. If we make a military project out of it, other nations will start emphasizing the military aspects of it, too. We could end up by making the weather a cause of war—cold or hot."

"But the Pentagon has a legitimate need to study weather control," I said. "There *are* military aspects to the situation."

"Of course there are!" Dr. Weis said, nodding vigorously. "And Major Vincent and his people are going about their work in the way that is best . . . for them. However, I'm concerned about a bigger picture—one that includes the military needs *and* all the other needs of the nation."

"So how do we stop the Pentagon?" Ted asked.

Dr. Weis took the pipe from his mouth. "We don't. Not directly, at least. The only way to prevent them from taking control of this idea is to go to Congress with a bigger idea."

"Bigger?"

Jim Dennis smiled. "I get it. Tell the Science Committee about a big, nonmilitary program that won't be classified, that will be spectacular, and that can get the Congressmen lots of publicity in their home districts."

Nodding, Dr. Weis said, "Exactly."

"A big project," I said.

"Spectacular," Ted added.

"And you have between now and the second week of January to figure it out," Jim Dennis told us.

Ted literally locked himself in his room at Climatology

for the next few weeks, while Tuli set himself up in business in a private office near Aeolus. Ted was furiously searching for a spectacular project to spring on Congress. Tuli was shuttling back and forth between Aeolus and the Manhattan Dome, trying to learn why the "air-conditioned island" was suffering from air pollution.

In the meantime, I chewed fingernails fretting over the upcoming Congressional hearings, Tuli's Security status, and everything else. It was really winter now, very snowy, as Ted had predicted, and bitterly cold. I thought sadly of the Islands every time I had to go outdoors.

Just before Christmas, Major Vincent called and invited us to Hanscom Air Force Base, where he was visiting for a few days. He sounded mysterious.

It was a gray, heavily cold day as I drove out to Climatology to pick up Ted. Then, together, we went to the Air Base. The major met us at the gate and guided us to the flight line next to one of the field's two-mile-long runways. We parked and sat huddled in the car as the warmth of the heater seeped away.

"What are we supposed to be seeing?" Ted asked.

"Wait a minute; it'll be here soon."

An air policeman, complete with white helmet and side-arm, walked over to check on us. When he saw the major he snapped into a salute.

A somber, featureless cloud deck had blanked out the sun, and a raw wind swooped out of the distant hills, unobstructed across the open sprawling airfield. The wind and dampness made it seem even colder than it really was, and the smoke from the Air Base's power generating station seemed almost to congeal in the heavy frigid air.

"What is this, an endurance test?" Ted growled.

Then we heard a plane overhead.

"Here she comes!" Major Vincent hopped out of the car.

As we followed him, he pointed to a distant speck that had just broken through the clouds. Quickly it grew to solid dimensions: an airplane circling the field once, twice, then lining up for a runway approach.

"Big one," Ted said as it made its final bank and glided down to the ground.

I could see multiwheeled landing gear extended from pods along her fuselage now. For a moment she seemed to hang in midair, as if reluctant to come back to earth. Then her tires screeched on the runway and she rolled toward us.

Ted was wrong, she wasn't big. She was immense. A huge, straight-winged, six-engined propjet, she loomed gigantically as she taxied to the flight line where we were standing, her turbos whining painfully in our ears. She looked like an ocean liner that had grown wings. Her tail soared impossibly high above us; her fuselage looked big enough to hold a whole city's bus fleet.

"She's brand new!" Major Vincent was practically bubbling with enthusiasm. "The first of a new series. This is her maiden flight—the Dromedary, we call her."

Ted shrugged. "One hump or two?"

"No humps. And no crew!"

That stirred Ted. "Landed automatically?"

"Right. This is the first time she's touched ground in three days. She's been aloft, flying automatically, for three days! That's classified information, by the way. Don't tell anyone who's not cleared."

"What's this got to do with. . . ." I started to ask.

But Ted was ahead of me. "She could be an unmanned

weather-observation plane . . . better than a satellite some ways because she's flying through the air you want to measure, instead of way above it. Could record temperatures, pressures, humidities, the works."

He looked up at the huge plane admiringly now. "How long has this been in the works? Can we go inside and look around? What instrumentation do you have on her? What about—"

The major held up his hands. "Okay, okay, come on aboard and check her out. She wasn't originally designed for weather observation, but some of our people think we can convert her to that mission."

"Great!" Ted beamed as we headed for the plane's forward hatch. "And she could carry plenty of seeding material for modification missions."

"I hadn't thought of that," Major Vincent said. "But I wanted you to see the plane. Working with the Pentagon won't be *all* red tape."

Ted glanced at me, and I could see our meeting with Dr. Weis flash into his mind. For once, though, he kept his silence.

He was still silent as we drove back through the late-afternoon darkness toward Boston.

"It looks as if the Pentagon is moving pretty fast on their weather project," I said.

Ted nodded. "Too fast. It's going to take something really big to get the ball away from 'em."

Without taking my eyes from the snaking line of red tail lights building up on the road ahead of us, I asked, "Do you have any ideas about what—"

"Hurricanes," Ted said, more to himself than to me.

"That's the only way to stop Vincent."

"What?"

"We've got to give Weis a big program that'll make weather control a front-page business and keep the Pentagon from gobbling it up. Hurricanes'll do it. We're going to stop hurricanes."

15. Pressure Systems

HURRICANES were the target, and Ted threw every ounce of his single-minded energy into working out a hurricane-stopping program for Dr. Weis. All through that snowy December we saw practically nothing of him. Barney had to just about drag him from his desk to spend Christmas day with us at Thornton.

Tuli, meanwhile, found the key to the Manhattan Dome's air-pollution problem. The Dome had created a temperature inversion within itself: warm air trapped at the top of the dome prevented the automobile and other engine smokes from rising high enough above the street level to let the Dome's blowers suck them out and purify the air.

"How will they fix that?" I asked when he explained it to me.

"It won't be too difficult, now that they know what the problem is," Tuli said. "They'll probably install suction vents at the street level to get the smog out before it builds up to noticeable proportions."

"That'll cost millions."

"I suppose it will," he said impassively. "It's a shame they built the Dome. In a few more years, Ted might be ready to air-condition the entire country . . . without plastic domes."

Aeolus made a handsome profit on Tuli's work, and he seemed pleased with his consulting job. But now there was hardly anything for him to do. Suspended by Climatology, idle at Aeolus, he began working nights with Ted on the hurricane idea.

Two days before the year ended, Ted called and asked me to come to his apartment after dinner. I wasn't surprised to meet Barney walking down the snowbank-lined street as I approached the place.

Tuli was there already, of course, straddling a turned-around kitchenette chair, his arms crossed on its back and his chin resting on his sleeves. He looked like a brooding Mongol horseman. Ted was pacing restlessly across the cramped little room.

"Glad you guys came," he said as we took off our coats and dropped them on a chair. "Want to try out this idea before calling Weis about it."

Barney and I sat on the tattered sofa.

"We *guys* are all ears," she said.

Ted grinned at her. "Okay," he said, still pacing, "here it is. There're two ways to stop a hurricane: dissipate it, or keep it out at sea, away from the coast. Up to now, all the hurricane researchers've been trying to break up the storms —dissipate 'em by knocking their energy balances out of whack. . . ."

"They try to seed the storms, don't they?" I asked.

"Right. But it's like tossing snowballs at an iceberg. All the seeding in the world won't dent a full-grown hurricane."

"There's even some evidence," Barney said, "that the hurricane absorbs the seeding energy."

Tuli agreed. "And uses it to add to the total windpower."

"Then you can't dissipate hurricanes," I said.

"Check. Too big for us, too much energy. They just blow along until natural forces break 'em up . . . and we can't match natural energy sources, not by a long shot. So we can't use our muscles. Got to use our brains."

He paused for a moment; then, "If we knew enough about hurricanes—their exact paths, their energy distributions, lots more—we could set up weather patterns that'd keep the storms out at sea. It's a tricky business, and we don't know how to do it yet. Predicting a storm's path is rough . . . lots of second-, third-, even fourth-order effects. A drop in pressure over Chicago might be the difference between a direct hit on Hatteras or a clean miss of the entire seacoast."

"But we're getting close to the point where we *can* predict storm tracks," Barney objected.

"Yeah, but we're not there yet. So we try another trick. Dissipate the storm *before* it's a hurricane. Even before it's a real storm . . . strangle it at birth, while it's still only a tropical disturbance."

"Can you do that?"

Ted nodded. "I think Tuli and I have figured it out."

"Tell Jerry the whole story," Tuli insisted. "There are dozens of tropical disturbances for each hurricane that eventually develops. We must either destroy each disturbance or risk having some of them develop into hurricanes. . . ."

"We can predict which ones'll develop," Ted said.

"With what accuracy? Fifty percent? You'll still have

to modify twice as many disturbances as there will be storms. The costs will be astronomical."

"Not compared to the damage a hurricane causes when it hits!"

I said, "Yes, that's the cost you're working against."

"So that's the bones of the idea: hit the tropical disturbances, stop 'em from developing into hurricanes. But only the ones that might develop into big storms, and only if their predicted storm tracks smell of coming close to the coast.

"Meanwhile we'll be learning how to set up weather patterns that'll keep hurricanes away from the shore. When we finish, we won't have to bother with knocking out disturbances—we'll know how to control the weather well enough to keep hurricanes out at sea!"

We sat there for a moment, digesting the idea in total silence, while Ted stood in the middle of the floor, his fists planted firmly on hips, looking like a world champion daring a challenger to raise his head.

We talked it over until the sky outside began to brighten. There were a million problems, a million unanswered questions. But Ted had made up his mind, and all we were doing was forcing him to think up answers that he could use later on Dr. Weis.

I drove Barney back to her apartment.

"I wonder about this idea," she said. "It's got more publicity value than science in it."

"What do you mean?"

"Smothering tropical disturbances . . . it's just brute force. It's just something Ted thought up to allow Dr. Weis to start a civilian weather-control project, instead of letting Major Vincent have a military one. Is this the way history is made? By dreaming up fancy projects?"

"No," I said. "History is made by individual men and women who do things. Sometimes they're right, and sometimes they're wrong. But it's the doing that makes history."

The snowbanks piled high in the cities and turned brown and rotten, until fresh snow whitened them again. The first week of January saw a temporary warm spell, but then a high-pressure mass of northern air slid silently into New England. Marked only by a brief flurry of snow, the northern High was barely cooler than the air it displaced. But it was dry and cloudless, heavy and still. That night the stars looked down on the half-thawed countryside while the warmth of the day radiated out of the ground and away into space, sending thermometers plummeting toward zero. By morning there was ice wherever thawing had appeared the previous day, and people who had been smiling at the thought of an early spring shook their heads and reached for the rock salt.

Ted was like a caged tiger when the Congressional hearings began. Dr. Weis had taken the hurricane-killing idea without too much comment, other than to say he'd "run it past my advisory committees." Meanwhile, both he and Jim Dennis cautioned Ted not to show up at the hearings.

"Most of the Committee members," Jim told us, "would be suspicious of a brilliant young genius. It's hard to admit to yourself that someone younger than you can be a whole lot smarter."

Ted reluctantly agreed, but I decided to keep a careful watch on him, and enlisted Barney and Tuli to help.

The Committee hearings began with Major Vincent and

his people explaining the need for a military weather-control project. The press gave them tremendous publicity, and the hearings were on television every morning. Meanwhile, Dr. Weis called with the news that the hurricane-killing idea had passed through his advisers with flying colors. He suggested that Dr. Barneveldt testify before the Congressional Committee about it. So Ted got busy briefing Dr. Barneveldt about THUNDER.

Just who named the idea THUNDER is a mystery we'll probably never clear up. Someone in the Washington maze of people and committees came up with it; it stood for Threatening *HU*rricane Neutralization, *DE*struction, and Recording. Ted grumbled something unintelligible when he first heard the title, but Project THUNDER became the official name.

The day Dr. Rossman was scheduled to appear before the Committee, Tuli and I just happened to drop in on Ted at his Climatology lair. And a good thing we did.

Barney came by to watch the session on Ted's TV set. Dr. Rossman, looking very dour and unhappy, chose to agree with Major Vincent all the way down the line. Military needs for weather control were extremely important, he said. Possibly just as important as the military need for missiles and space stations. The Climatology Division, he made clear, was ready to do whatever the Pentagon wanted.

Ted leaped out of his desk chair as though he was going to smash the television set.

"He's sold out! He figured that Weis can't beat the Pentagon, so he's lining up with Vincent!"

"No, wait Ted. Maybe—"

"He knows I'm against the military game," Ted raged, "so he's trying to get rid of me by backing them!"

There wasn't anything we could do to calm him down. We were lucky to keep him from jumping onto the next tube train and storming into the Committee hearing with a flaming sword.

We took Ted to dinner that evening, and stayed with him far into the night. Dr. Barneveldt was scheduled to appear before the Committee the following day, and this was about the only thing that calmed him down. He spent an hour on the phone to Washington, talking to Dr. Barneveldt in his hotel room, giving him some last-minute points about Project THUNDER.

Tuli went straight to Climatology with Ted the next day, and I made sure to get there in time for the telecast of the hearing.

Even on the small screen of the portable TV you could see that Dr. Barneveldt obviously impressed the Committee members. His Nobel Prize awed them in advance, and as he sat at the witness desk, before a battery of microphones, he looked like a Congressman's idea of a scientist. He seemed to sense this, for he played his role to the hilt.

After agreeing that there were important military applications for weather control, Dr. Barneveldt went on to say:

"But there are equally important—no, more important— needs for this new knowledge in the peacetime, civilian world. It would be a pity if the short-term needs of the military obscured the long-term benefits that weather control can bring to all mankind. If man can control his weather, he may be able to avert many of the causes of war. Poverty, disease, hunger . . . all these are immensely influenced by climate and weather. Imagine a world where there is no lack of water, where crops flourish every year, where disastrous floods and storms are a thing of the past."

Jim Dennis, from his seat at the Committee members' table, leaned forward to ask: "Can this kind of thing be done now?"

Dr. Barneveldt hesitated dramatically. He seemed to be enjoying the television limelight. "It is possible to begin work toward that goal. Some of my colleagues at the Climatology Division and elsewhere, for example, have evolved a technique that could possibly prevent hurricanes from threatening our shores. . . ."

The rest was lost in a stampede by the newsmen for the phones. By evening Project THUNDER was the biggest scientific news since the moon landings. But it was a Washington story: Dr. Weis and Dr. Barneveldt were the "experts." Ted and the rest of us stayed in Boston, grateful for once that Rossman had kept us out of the public eye.

The Science Committee hearings went on for weeks, but it was clear that Project THUNDER had at least pulled up to a neck-and-neck position with Major Vincent's plan for a military weather-control program. Most of the Congressmen made it look as if they wanted both a military and civilian project.

In effect, the Committee dropped the Pentagon vs. THUNDER problem into the hands of the Administration. Which was right where Dr. Weis wanted it, since he was the White House's adviser in scientific and technical matters. So it came as no surprise when, early in March, Dr. Weis invited Ted and me to his White House office.

Cyclogenesis: the birth of a storm. Mix equal parts of moist maritime air and frigid polar air. Stir well in a counterclockwise motion. Place the cyclonic storm over Cape Hatteras in early

March and watch closely. Obeying the logic of the sun's energy input, the earth's spin, the winds and waters and lands around it, the storm moves northward along the Atlantic seaboard. In the Carolinas it drops freezing rain and sleet, but as it moves into Virgina, with more polar air feeding into it from aloft, the precipitation turns to huge, wet dollops of snow. Washington is buried in white, while farther north—in Philadelphia, New York, and Boston—armies of men and machines begin to mass for the coming attack, and hope they can prevent their cities from being paralyzed by the blizzard.

When Ted and I took the tube train in Boston, the sky was still clear. But Washington, we knew, would be in the middle of the blizzard as we pulled into the terminal. Even underground you could see the effects of the weather: people jammed the capital terminal, late for work, upset, some even angry. Those coming down the escalators from the street had shoulders and hats crusted with the heavy, sticky snow. Boots left wet, sloppy trails everywhere. Underground slideways were choked with people.

Ted insisted on going topside and walking the few blocks between the terminal and the White House. Nothing was moving on the city streets; even the surface slideways were shut down. The few struggling pedestrians had to bend over nearly double against the howling wind. The snow was thick and heavy underfoot, and in half a minute I was as cold as I ever want to be—even inside my sturdiest coat, boots, gloves, and fur-lined hat.

Ted loved it. "With a couple of platoons of ski troops we could take over the Government!"

"You can have it," I mumbled from behind my turned-up collar, "on a day like this."

"Don't worry, it'll be over in an hour or so. Blowing north. We'll run into it in Boston again tonight."

"Nice timing."

Dr. Weis' office was an airy, spacious room in the White House executive wing, with French windows that looked out over the blizzard-smothered lawn.

"At least it's warm in here," he said as he gestured us to chairs. "You two looked as if you'd walked all the way from Boston when you came in!"

"I feel as if we did," I answered.

Ted laughed.

"I want to give you a firsthand report on where we stand with THUNDER," Dr. Weis said, rocking back slightly in his big, padded chair.

"Before you do," Ted interrupted, "you ought to know about the coming hurricane season. Ran a few preliminary checks last week. Kind of shaky, but it looks as if it'll be the same kind of season as last year. Same number of storms, roughly. If we let 'em develop, that is."

Dr. Weis reached for a pipe from the rack on his desk. "The prospect of killing hurricanes is very attractive, although extremely expensive. It's about the only thing that can stand up to the pressure the Pentagon's been putting on in Cabinet meetings."

"It's gotten to that level," I said.

"Indeed it has," Dr. Weis puffed his pipe alight. "But I think we have the edge. I've been claiming that hurricane killing will help Major Vincent and his people to learn some of the basic things they must know before they can start weather-modification experiments. So, in a sense, THUNDER isn't stopping the Pentagon, it will be helping them."

"Wait a minute," Ted said. "Hurricane killing is only part of the show . . . and we'll be killing tropical disturbances, not full-grown storms."

"Yes, I know."

"But the real aim of the Project is to learn how to control the weather well enough to steer hurricanes away from the coast. We'll only hunt out tropical disturbances and smother 'em until we get smart enough to control the hurricanes."

"That's what I wanted to talk to you about," Dr. Weis said. "This weather-control part of the scheme has drawn a considerable amount of criticism. And it's come from several different sources."

"But that's——"

"Now hear me out, Ted." Dr. Weis hunched forward and leaned his arms on the desk. "You admit that you don't know enough to control the weather so that hurricanes will be kept away from our coasts. And even if you did, you'd have to control the weather over most of the continental United States. . . ."

"And Canada."

He nodded. "And Mexico, too, I'll warrant."

"Sure. So what?"

"It's politically dangerous. Explosive. Too much of a chance that something might go wrong. Suppose you made a mistake? The consequences could be disastrous."

"Now wait," Ted shot back. "What do you think we want to do, divert the Mississippi through Arizona? We'll control the weather, sure, but not enough to cause disasters. Couldn't, even if we wanted to! Too much energy involved. We're not going to make it snow in California or thaw out Alaska."

"You and I know that, Ted, but what about the average voter? Lots of people get sore at the Weather Bureau when their picnics are rained out, or their crops get damaged. Do you realize what political dynamite it would be for the Government to accept the responsibility for controlling the weather?"

"It was a political bombshell to declare independence in 1776, too. Some things've got to be done!"

"Weather control will eventually become a reality," Dr. Weis replied, his voice a trifle higher and more nasal. "But you can't jump into it too quickly. Project THUNDER—the hurricane-killing part of it, that is—is an excellent beginning. After a year or two of successful demonstrations, we'll be ready to try the next step. And, more important, the country will be psychologically prepared."

"But we can do it now, this year! All we need is some time to check out the theories and we're ready to swing it."

"Technically ready, but not politically. And even on the technical side, the earliest operations in weather control will be little more than educated gambles."

Ted slammed a fist on the arm of his chair. "Look, I don't know what you're scared of. It rains and snows on people now. We have floods and droughts. So the Government steps in and gets blamed for 'em by a few weirdos and nuts. So what? How about the droughts the Government gets credit for stopping, or the floods that never happen, or the bumper crops that controlled weather can give you?"

Dr. Weis leaned back and shook his head. "Ted, you understand science, but not politics. It just doesn't work that way."

"Well, THUNDER isn't going to work without weather control. It'll be a waste of time and effort without it."

"You won't accept the Project without the weather-control feature of it?"

Ted said stiffly, "Killing the tropical disturbances is a dead end, a stopgap. Unless it leads us into real weather control, it's the wrong way to fight hurricanes."

Dr. Weis got up from his chair. "Well, come on, we've talked long enough. Let's get this thing resolved."

"What now, another committee?"

"No," he answered, glancing at his desk clock. "We don't give all our problems to committees. Come with me."

We followed him down a corridor and up a flight of stairs. We went through an unmarked door into a large, oval-shaped office that was dominated by a broad desk covered with papers and three phones of different colors. Behind the unoccupied desk was a pair of flags.

I looked at Ted. He seemed to realize whose office it was just as I did.

The door on the other side of the room opened and the President stepped briskly to his desk.

"Hello," he said. "You must be Mr. Marrett and Mr. Thorn."

He shook hands with us, his grip strong. He was taller than I had thought him to be, and looked younger than his TV image. He gestured us to the chairs before his desk. As we sat down, he tapped some of the papers on his desk.

"Can you actually stop hurricanes?"

"Yes, sir," Ted answered at once.

The President smiled. "There's no doubt in your mind at all?"

"We can do it, sir, if you'll give us the tools."

"You understand, don't you, that the Defense Department has also proposed a weather project? If I buck the Secretary of Defense on this, it could create ammunition for the opposition this November."

"Hurricanes could be a voting issue all along the Atlantic seaboard," Ted answered, "and the Gulf Coast."

With a grin, the President said, "I didn't do too well along the Gulf Coast last election. And if you fail to stop the hurricanes, I'll do even worse. On the other hand, if I don't give the go-ahead for Project THUNDER, hurricanes will remain strictly nonpolitical."

Ted didn't reply.

"Something else has come up," Dr. Weis said. "Ted here feels that the Project should really be aimed at the broader goal of controlling the weather across the United States, rather than just stopping hurricanes."

"Controlling the weather." The President turned from his Science Adviser to look squarely at Ted. "That seems . . . fantastic. The weather is so violent, so vast and wild. I can't imagine man ever controlling it."

"We can do it," Ted answered firmly. "It only looks wild and violent because you don't understand it. There's logic to the weather; it obeys physical laws, just like an apple falling off a tree. We're starting to learn what those laws are; once we've learned enough, we can control the weather. Just like fire—once it was wild and dangerous and mysterious. But man learned to tame it. We still don't know everything there is to know about it, but fire's as commonplace as sneezing."

The President pursed his lips thoughtfully. "So there's a

logic to the weather? Certainly there's a beauty to it, even when it's storming. Tell me, Mr. Marrett, do you know enough about the weather's logic to be to tell when this snow's going to stop? I have to fly to Chicago this afternoon."

Ted grinned. Looking at his wristwatch, he said, "Should be stopped now."

"You're sure?" the President asked, turning toward the window drapes.

Nodding, Ted answered, "It's got to be."

The President pulled the drapes open. The sky was dazzling blue, with just a few departing clouds. The sun sparkled off the heaped snowdrifts across the lawn.

"You apparently know what you're talking about," he said. "But controlling the weather is a big step. A very big step."

"I know," Ted replied. Then, speaking slowly and very carefully, he explained, "With full-scale weather control, the cost of keeping the country free of hurricane damage will probably be lower than it would be if we had to hunt out every threatening disturbance in the ocean and kill it. And weather control is the ultimate objective. It's going to be done sooner or later. . . . I'd like to see it done now, by this Administration."

"I hope to be here another four years," the President replied laughingly.

Ted went on to repeat most of the arguments he had used with Dr. Weis; the Science Adviser went through his counterargument, too. The President sat back and listened.

Finally, he said, "Mr. Marrett, I appreciate your dedication and drive. But you must remember that the Government bears the responsibility for the well-being of the whole nation. It sounds to me as if your ideas might work. But they've never been tested on the scale that you yourself said would have to be done. If you're wrong, we could lose much more than an election; we could lose lives and a staggering amount of property and resources."

"That's true, sir," Ted said. "But if I'm right...."

"You'll still be right next year, won't you? I like Project THUNDER. I think stopping hurricanes will be a tremendous gift to the nation . . . and a big enough job for the first year out. Are you willing to settle for that part of it, and let weather control wait for a while?"

Nodding glumly, Ted said, "If that's the way it's got to be."

The President turned to Dr. Weis. "We'll still be sticking our necks out, you realize. THUNDER is something of a risk, and going against the Pentagon isn't always good politics."

"But the return could be immense," Dr. Weis said.

"Yes, I realize that. And I suppose the benefits of stopping even one hurricane are more important than a few million votes this fall."

Dr. Weis shrugged. "Politics is an art, Mr. President. I'm only a scientist."

He laughed. "We'll make a politician out of you yet. You're strongly in favor of THUNDER?"

"Of the hurricane-stopping part of it, yes."

"Strongly in favor?"

"Strongly, sir," Dr. Weis said.

"All right, then. If Congress will authorize the funds, let's go ahead with it."

We chatted for a few minutes more, and the President even kidded me about my Massachusetts uncles working for his opponent last election. I quickly told him that Father had been on his side. The President's secretary came in and reminded him of the next appointment, and we were politely ushered out of the office after another round of handshakes.

"Good luck with THUNDER," the President said to us as we left. "I'll be watching your progress closely."

Ted nodded. Outside in the corridor, he muttered "We'd make a lot more progress if he'd bought all of THUNDER instead of just the safe part."

16. Project THUNDER

It WAS a wild four months. Between March and July we had to organize a project that involved Air Force planes, Navy ships, NASA satellites, and a good percentage of the Weather Bureau's talent and equipment. The Project staff was drawn mainly from Ted's small group at Climatology and my people at Aeolus. I was also in charge of hiring new people, who officially worked for Aeolus, but actually were THUNDER personnel. And, since the Project was not a military one, Barney and Tuli were free to work with us.

Finally, the first week of July, we were ready to leave for Miami. Dr. Barneveldt saw us off at Logan Airport, together with a crowd of newsmen and photographers. We were no longer hidden from the public view; in fact, there was a major news conference scheduled for later that afternoon, in Miami.

After a few final words of parting, we took off in the executive jet. Inside it, we still had work to do. I was reviewing a draft of our agreement with the British government concerning the island of Bermuda. Ted had decided that

THUNDER would protect the mainland of North America and the Caribbean islands; but he wanted to leave the open-ocean storms alone. He had two reasons. First, he needed a scientific control on the THUNDER experiments, and the storms we didn't touch could be used as a comparison against those we worked on. Second, we simply didn't have the resources to tackle every disturbance in the whole ocean.

But storms that stayed well away from the mainland still threatened Bermuda, so we had worked out an agreement with the British that Bermuda would not be protected.

While I read through the State Department's paperwork, Ted and Barney, across the aisle from me, were talking about the press conference we would be facing that afternoon.

"It's important to give the newsmen the correct impression," Barney was saying. "We've got to show them that THUNDER is strictly an experiment."

Ted nodded impatiently.

I looked up from my reading. "Ted, don't forget that Dr. Weis is going to be right there on the platform with you. You'd better not say anything that sounds like weather control."

He shot me a surly glance.

"And don't try to predict the future," Barney added. "Just talk about the work we're going to do for the Project. Don't let the newsmen work you into a position where you're making any promises. . . ."

He threw up his hands. "Maybe I ought to put on a false beard and dark glasses and sneak away before the press conference starts! Listen, you know as well as I do that either we produce results with THUNDER or get booted out. Don't try to hedge it. No matter how much we jabber, everybody knows that if we let one hurricane get through and cause damage, we're dead. We've got to throw a shut-out."

Tuli popped up from the seat behind Ted. "We won't be able to stop every hurricane. Not unless the disturbances are spaced apart well enough so that we can work on just one or two at a time. At the height of the season, when the disturbances come in groups, some of them will get past us."

"That's right," Barney agreed. Turning back to Ted, she urged, "We've got to be cautious, especially in front of the newsmen."

"If we were cautious," Ted grumbled, "we wouldn't be on this plane right now."

One of the plush Miami Beach hotels had been chosen for the press conference. The main ballroom was jammed, and under the television lights we all felt hot and edgy.

The chief of the Miami Weather Bureau office intro-duced us with a long, rambling speech. "Brilliant young men . . . challenging new ideas . . . youthful daring. . . ." Ted sat slumped back in his seat, glowering like a thunder-head: powerful, looming, dangerous.

When the Miami chief finally finished, Dr. Weis gave the main pitch. In his careful way he reminded everyone about the hurricanes that had hit the mainland United States the previous year, and of the billions in damage they had cost. (While he spoke, most of the Florida tourist trade was piling into the airports and terminals, leaving for safer areas until after the hurricane season.)

ELTING MEMORIAL LIBRARY
93 MAIN STREET
NEW PALTZ, N. Y.

"If we can successfully stop even one hurricane that would hit the coast," Dr. Weis went on, "the savings in storm damage—not to mention human lives—will more than pay for the cost of the entire Project."

After a detailed review of THUNDER's organization— and paying due credit to ESSA, the Defense Department, the Coast Guard, the Congress, and every other Government organization that had anything to do with land, sea or air (he even mentioned Aeolus)—Dr. Weis asked for questions from the newsmen.

They had plenty. And after five minutes, they realized that Ted was their key to a good story; they kept shooting their questions at him. Finally, one of the newsmen asked:

"There've been a lot of weather-modification trials in the past, but this is really the Government's first large-scale weather-control program, isn't it?"

Dr. Weis took the microphone on the table in his hands and answered before Ted could. "Project THUNDER is not a weather-control program. This is merely an experiment, and a limited one at that, despite its size. The Project will attempt to modify tropical disturbances that might grow into hurricanes that would threaten populated areas. That's all that will be done. No other aspect of anyone's weather will be touched, and we will not *control* the weather, by any stretch of the imagination."

Ted looked down the long table at the Science Adviser, then turned to his microphone. "The Government isn't ready for weather control. Not yet, anyway. Most of us on THUNDER would love to try a full-scale weather-control program. In fact, real weather control would be a lot better as far as keeping hurricanes off your doorstep is concerned."

"I wouldn't phrase it quite that way," Dr. Weis said,

fumbling with his pipe. "Project THUNDER is a very exciting first step toward eventual control of the weather. But——"

"But we're restricted to working on disturbances while they're out at sea . . . we're not trusted with changing the weather over the United States."

Dr. Weis' face was changing color. "You've got to learn to walk before you can run. You haven't demonstrated that you can modify the disturbances yet. With good luck—and patience—you'll get to weather control in due time."

Ted shrugged. "I think the due time could be this year. We've already learned to walk. We can run as far as we have to . . . if the Government'd let us."

One of the newsmen called out, "Mr. Marrett—after this hurricane season is over, say around election day, how will we be able to judge the success of Project THUNDER?"

Ted shut his eyes momentarily, like a man about to plunge from a great height. "If any part of mainland America or the Caribbean islands suffers loss of life or property damage from a hurricane—THUNDER will have failed."

There was an eternal moment of shocked silence.

I felt my jaw go slack. No one could live up to that guarantee! Ted glared down the table at the rest of us, as if daring anyone to contradict him. The newsmen scrambled for the phones.

The evening headlines summed it up neatly:

NO HURRICANES TO HIT U.S.,
VOWS STORM CONTROL CHIEF

Dr. Weis exploded. He raked Ted over the coals for three

hours before flying back to Washington. He threatened to cancel the entire Project, or at least fire Ted and replace him with someone else. But the damage had been done. And Ted stubbornly insisted:

"It's the truth. We're here to stop hurricanes. No matter how many we stop, if one gets through, everyone'll think we've flopped. Nobody's going to be satisfied with a hurricane-killing project that doesn't kill hurricanes. One storm gets through and we're dead. Why hide it?"

So we went to work, setting up Project headquarters in a prefab building on the Miami city waterfront that the Navy loaned us. But Ted's promise hung over us like a death knell.

By the end of July the first hurricane took shape.

Fifteen hundred miles east of Florida and two hundred feet underwater, a school of bonito as numerous as the human population of Miami suddenly veered from a menacing form bearing down on them. Larger than a cachalot whale or even a giant blue, the submarine slid darkly through the crowded sea, sampling water temperatures and reporting them every half hour to THUNDER headquarters. An unmanned Dromedary patrol plane droned automatically across the mid-Atlantic sky, continuously measuring atmospheric conditions and relaying the information to the Project. The plane and submarine crossed paths. A technician in THUNDER's data-reduction section watched curiously as one of the big computers rattled to life. He took a fast look at the cryptic words and symbols being printed out, then reached for the nearest phone. A low-pressure trough with cool air mixing into it, a warm column of air at the center rising straight up to the tropopause, and upwelling water beneath the disturbance. A hurricane was being born.

We dubbed the first storm Andrea. It stayed out in mid-ocean, so we didn't have to attempt modifying it. The hurricane was a living laboratory for us, though; we followed its course minute by minute, and sent squadrons of planes into it to measure and sample every facet of its make-up. Andrea blew close to Bermuda, but with our advanced warning of its path, the islanders held damage to a minimum.

Bettina turned up hard on the heels of the first storm, developing practically overnight in the Caribbean. We caught her in time—barely—and kept Bettina down to a small tropical storm. She never neared hurricane force, although she caused trouble enough wherever her gale winds and heavy rains hit.

"Close," Ted muttered as the results of our work on Bettina showed up on the big plotting screen that dominated THUNDER's main control center. "Another couple of hours and we'd've been too late. Got to do better."

We learned fast. The hurricane season was really getting started now, and we were faced with dozens of tropical disturbances. We sharpened our techniques and honed our teams to a fine fighting edge. Dr. Weis called practically every day, but we had no time to worry. We worked, we ate, we slept, and then worked some more. Time became a dizzy spiral of finding, fighting, and killing tropical disturbances.

Ted was acting strangely, though. He was away from THUNDER headquarters almost as much as he was with us. I kept track of him by reading his expense vouchers: Cape Kennedy, Boston, Washington, Kansas City—he even spent a weekend up in the Atlantic Station satellite (which cost the Project eighteen thousand dollars; orbital flights were still expensive).

But whenever we faced a really tough job, Ted would show up to direct the battle. Sometimes he was hustling toward his desk with his travelkit in one hand and his dirty laundry in the other, but he was always there when the chips were down.

"What are all these trips about?" I asked him one evening. The watch at control center was changing shifts, and Barney, Ted, and I were eating a dinner of cold sandwiches and soda at his desk.

"Been visiting people who can help us," he said, between gulps of a sandwich.

"In Kansas City?"

He grinned. "They've got meteorologists in K.C."

"Isn't that a bit inland for hurricane control?" Barney asked. She was as curious as I.

"Look, I'm not talking about THUNDER to these guys. It's weather control. Sooner or later, we're going to need all the brains and help we can get . . . when we start controlling the weather across the country."

"But you're not going to do any weather-control work until THUNDER is proved successful," I said.

"Why wait?" he snapped. "Weis and his committees want to go slow. If THUNDER flops, it's back to the labs for all of us. Even if THUNDER succeeds, what d'you think they're going to do?" Before we could answer he went on, "They'll want to do THUNDER all over again next year. And maybe every year. Hurricane control is great . . . but not this way. Even if it works. I'm shooting for weather control, no matter what."

Barney glanced at me, then said, "I don't understand how your trips around the country are helping us toward weather control, Ted."

"When this hurricane season's over, I want to hit Weis and Dennis and the others with a solid story on weather control. I'm getting as many people on our side as possible. I want to show 'em in Washington that there's a big-league team ready to go."

"But what happens if THUNDER fails?" I asked. "And all we need is one hurricane to kill us."

"We haven't flopped yet."

"But the hardest part of the season is just starting," Barney said.

"I know. We're holding our own so far. Tuli and his people are doing a little work on the side for me . . . nothing much, not taking many people off the regular Project work. But we're getting enough data on the storms and their weather patterns to start thinking about some honest weather control. You know, keep 'em off the coast by controlling the weather across the continent."

"Weather-control research?" I said. "If Dr. Weis finds out . . ."

"Don't let him. And Barney, give Tuli all the computer time he needs."

"We're running twenty-four hours a day as it is," she said. "We'll have to time-share with more computers somewhere else."

"Okay, do it. But keep Tuli's stuff on our own machines; don't let it out of the Project."

"Ted, I don't like this," I said. "We've got the hardest part of the season ahead of us. Tuli warned us that there'll be situations when there're simply too many disturbances for us to hit all at the same time. We know from experience now that we can't run more than two or three missions a day . . . we simply don't have enough men and equipment for more than that. And now you're taking valuable men off the real work of the Project to do research we have no business doing. . . ."

"Hey, whose side are you on anyway? This research is for weather control, buddy, and that's what we're shooting for. Not hurricane tinkering. THUNDER's only a drop in the bucket compared to what we can really do."

"But if you don't get that first drop into the bucket, what then?"

He frowned. "Okay, so we're gambling. But let's gamble big. Shoot for the jackpot."

We could have argued all night. But it wouldn't have budged him a millimeter. And the biggest argument of all was brewing out on the Atlantic as we sat there at Ted's desk.

It took a few more days for the facts to show up on THUNDER's giant plotting screen. But when they did make themselves clear, we knew that all our dreams were going to come crashing down in the howling wind of a mammoth hurricane.

17. Hurricane Fury

∿∿∿∿∿∿∿∿∿∿∿∿

THE viewscreen map that loomed over Ted's desk at THUNDER control center showed our battlefield: all of North America and the North Atlantic Ocean, including the coasts of Europe and Africa. As September entered its final ten days, we saw disturbances mushrooming all across the ocean. Most of them we left alone, since they weren't threatening. One of them developed into a hurricane, which we called Nora, that stayed well out at sea.

Then the day that Tuli warned about finally arrived.

Ted gathered us around his desk, with the giant viewscreen staring down our throats. Hurricane Nora was howling up the mid-Atlantic; she was no trouble. But four tropical disturbances, marked by red danger symbols, were strung out along the fifteenth parallel from the Antilles Islands to the Cape Verdes.

"There's the story," Ted told us, prowling nervously along the foot of the viewscreen. Gesturing toward the map, he said, "Nora's okay, won't even bother Bermuda much. But these four Lows'll bug us for sure."

Tuli shook his head. "We can't handle all four of them at once. One, possibly two, will get past us."

Ted looked sharply at him, then turned to me. "How about it, Jerry? What's the logistics picture?"

"Tuli's right," I admitted. "The planes and crews have been working around the clock for the past couple of weeks and we just don't have enough—"

"Skip the flute music. How many of these Lows can we hit?"

Shrugging, I answered, "Two. Maybe three, if we really push it."

Barney was standing beside me. "The computer just finished an updated statistical analysis of the four disturbances. Their storm tracks all threaten the East Coast. The two closest ones have point-eight probabilities of reaching hurricane strength. The farther pair are only point-five."

"Fifty-fifty for the last two," Ted muttered. "But they've got the longest time to develop. Chances'll be better for 'em by tomorrow."

"It's those two closest disturbances that are the most dangerous," Barney said. "They each have an eighty percent chance of turning into hurricanes that will hit us."

"We can't stop them all," Tuli said. "What will we do, Ted?"

Before Ted could answer, his phone buzzed. He leaned across the desk and punched the button. "Dr. Weis calling from Washington," the operator said.

He grimaced. "Okay, put him on." Sliding into his desk chair, Ted waved us back to our posts as Dr. Weis' worried face came on the phone screen.

"I've just seen this morning's weather map," the President's Science Adviser said, with no preliminaries. "It looks as if you're in trouble."

"Got our hands full," Ted said evenly.

I started back for my own cubicle. I could hear Dr. Weis' voice, a little edgier than usual, saying, "The opposition has turned THUNDER into a political issue, with less than six weeks to the election. If you hadn't made the newsmen think that you could stop every hurricane. . . ."

The rest was lost in the chatter and bustle of the control center. The one room filled the entire second floor of our headquarters building. It was a frenetic conglomeration of people, desks, calculating machines, plotting boards, map printers, cabinets, teletypes, phones, viewscreens, and endless piles of paper—with the huge viewscreen map hanging over it all. I made my way across the cluttered, windowless expanse and stepped into my glass-walled cubicle.

It was quiet inside, with the door closed. Phone screens lined the walls, and half my desk was covered with a private switchboard that put me in direct contact with a network of THUNDER support stations ranging from New Orleans to the Atlantic Satellite Station, in synchronous orbit some twenty-three thousand miles above the mouth of the Amazon River.

I looked across the control center again, and saw Ted still talking earnestly into the phone. There was work to be done. I began tapping out phone numbers on my master switchboard, alerting the Navy and Air Force bases that were supporting the Project, trying to get ready to hit those hurricane threats as hard and as fast as we could.

While I worked, Ted finally got off the phone. Barney came over with a thick sheaf of computer print-out sheets;

probably the detailed analysis of the storm threats. As soon as I could break away, I went over and joined them.

"Okay," Ted was saying, "if we leave those two farther-out Lows alone, they'll develop into hurricanes overnight. We can knock 'em out now without much sweat, but by tomorrow they'll be too big for us."

"The same applies to the two closest disturbances," Barney pointed out. "And they're much closer and already developing fast. . . ."

"We'll have to skip one of 'em. The first one—off the Leewards—is too close to ignore. So we'll hit Number One, skip the second, and hit Three and Four."

Barney took her glasses off. "That won't work, Ted. If we don't stop the second one now, by tomorrow it will be—"

"A walloping big hurricane. I know." He made a helpless gesture. "But if we throw enough stuff at Number Two to smother it, we'll have to leave Three and Four alone until tomorrow. In the meantime, they'll both develop and we'll have two brutes on our hands!"

"But this one. . . ."

"There's a chance that if we knock out the closest Low, Number Two'll change its track and head out to sea."

"That's a terribly slim chance. The numbers show—"

"Okay, it's a slim chance. But it's all we've got to work with."

"Isn't there anything else we can do?" she asked. "If a hurricane strikes the coast. . . ."

"Weis is already looking through his mail for my resignation," Ted said. "Okay, we're in trouble. Best we can manage is hit Number One, skip Two, and wipe out Three and Four before they get strong enough to make waves."

Barney looked down at the numbers on the computer sheets. "That means we're going to have a full-grown hurricane heading for Florida within twenty-four hours."

"Look," Ted snapped, "we can sit around here debating 'til they *all* turn into hurricanes. Let's scramble. Jerry, you heard the word. Get the planes up."

I dashed back to my cubicle and sent out the orders. A few minutes later, Barney came by. Standing dejectedly in the doorway, she asked herself out loud:

"Why did he agree to take on this Project? He knows it's not the best way to handle hurricanes. It's too chancy, too expensive. We're working ourselves to death. . . ."

"So are the aircrews," I answered. "And the season's just starting to hit its peak."

"Then why did he have to make the newsmen think we could run up a perfect score the first year?"

"Because he's Ted Marrett. He not only thinks he can control the weather, he thinks he owns it."

"There's no room in him for failure," she said. "If this storm does hit, and if the Project is canceled . . . what will it do to him?"

"What will it do to you?" I asked her.

She shook her head. "I don't know, Jerry. But I'm terribly afraid we're going to find out in another day or two."

Tropical storms are built on seemingly slight differences of air temperature. A half-dozen degrees of difference over an area hundreds of miles across can power the giant heat engine of a hurricane. Ted's method of smothering tropical disturbances before they reached hurricane strength was to smooth out the temperature difference between the core of the disturbances and their outer fringes.

The nearest disturbance was developing quickly. It had already passed over the Leeward Islands and entered the Caribbean by the time our first planes reached it. The core of the disturbance was a column of warm air shooting upward from the sea's surface to the tropopause, some ten miles high. Swirling around this column was relatively cooler air sliding into the low-pressure trough created by the warm column.

If the disturbance were left to itself, it would soak up moisture from the warm sea and condense it into rainfall. The heat released by this condensation would power winds of ever-mounting intensity. A cycle would be established: winds bring in moisture, the water vapor condenses into rain, the heat released builds up the wind's power. Finally, when the storm reached a certain intensity, centrifugal force would begin sucking down cooler air from very high altitudes. The cool air would be compressed and heated as it sank, and then fed into the massive cloud walls around the storm's core—which would now be the eye of a full-grown hurricane. A thousand megatons of energy would be on the loose, unstoppable, even by Project THUNDER.

Our job was to prevent that cycle from establishing itself. We had to warm up the air flowing into the disturbance and chill down its core until temperatures throughout the storm were practically the same. A heat engine with all its parts at the same temperature (or close to it) simply won't work.

As I started giving out orders for the three simultaneous missions, Tuli stuck his head into my office doorway.

"I'm off to see the dragon firsthand." He was grinning excitedly.

"Which one?"

"Number One dragon; it's in the Caribbean now."

"I know. Good luck. Bring back its ears."

He nodded, a round-faced, brown-skinned St. George going against the most destructive monster man had ever faced.

As I parceled out orders over the phones, a battery of gigajoule lasers aboard the Atlantic Station began pumping their energy into the northern peripheries of the budding storms. The lasers were similar to the type mounted in the Air Force's missile-defense satellites. They had been placed aboard the Atlantic Station at Ted's insistence, with the personal backing of Dr. Weis and the White House. Only carefully selected Air Force personnel were allowed near them. The entire section of the satellite station where they were installed was under armed guard, much to the discomfort of the civilians aboard.

Planes from a dozen airfields were circling the northern edges of the disturbances, sowing the air with rain-producing crystals.

"Got to seed for hours at a time," Ted once told me. "That's a mistake the early experimenters made—never stayed on the job long enough to force an effect on the weather."

I was watching the disturbance in the Caribbean. That was the closest threat, and the best developed of all the four disturbances. Radar plots, mapped on Ted's giant viewscreen, showed rain clouds expanding and showering precipitation over an ever-widening area. As the water vapor in the seeded air condensed into drops, the air temperature rose slightly. The satellite-borne lasers were also helping to heat the air feeding into the disturbance and confuse its circulation pattern.

It looked as if we were just making the disturbance bigger. But Ted and other technical staff people had figured out the energy balance in the young storm. They knew what they were doing. That didn't stop me from gnawing my lower lip, though.

Tuli was in an Air Force bomber, part of two squadrons of planes flying at staggered altitudes. From nearly sea level to fifty thousand feet, they roared into the central column of warm air in precise formation and began dumping tons of liquid nitrogen into the rising tropical air.

The effect was spectacular. The TV screens alongside the big plotting map showed what the planes saw: tremendous plumes of white sprang out behind each plane as the cryogenic liquid flash-froze the water vapor in the warm column. It looked as if some cosmic wind had suddenly spewed its frigid breath through the air. The nitrogen quickly evaporated, soaking up enormous quantities of heat. Most of the frozen vapor simply evaporated again, although the radar plots showed that some condensation and actual rainfall occurred.

I made my way to Ted's desk to check the results of the core freezing.

"Looks good," he was saying into the phone.

The teletype next to his desk chugged into life. It started printing a report from the observation planes that followed the bombers.

Ted stepped over and looked at the numbers. "Broke up

the core okay. Now if she doesn't reform, we can scratch Number One off the map."

It was evening before we could tell for sure. The disturbance's source of energy—the differing temperatures of the air masses it contained—had been taken away from it. The plotting screen showed a large swatch of concentric irregular isobars, like a lopsided bull's-eye, with a sullen red "L" marking the center of the low-pressure area, just north of Jamaica. The numbers on the screen showed a central pressure of 991 millibars, nowhere near that of a typical hurricane. Wind speeds had peaked at fifty-two knots and were dying off now. Kingston and Guantanamo were reporting moderate-to-heavy rain, but at Santo Domingo, six hundred miles to the east, it had already cleared.

The disturbance was just another small tropical storm, and a rapidly weakening one at that. The two farther disturbances, halfway out across the ocean, had been completely wiped out. The planes were on their way home. The laser crews aboard the Atlantic Station were recharging their energy storage coils.

"Shall I see if the planes can reload and fly another mission tonight?" I asked Ted. "Maybe we can still hit Number Two."

He shook his head. "Won't do any good. Look at her," he said, pointing to the viewscreen map. "By the time the planes could get to her, she'll be a full-grown hurricane. There's nothing we can do about it now."

18. Omega

So WE didn't sleep that night. We stayed at the control center and watched the storm develop on the TV picture beamed from the Atlantic Station. At night they had to use infrared cameras, of course, but we could still see—in the ghostly IR images—a broad spiral of clouds stretching across four hundred miles of open ocean.

Practically no one had left the control center, but the big room was deathly quiet. Even the chattering calculating machines and teletypes seemed to have stopped. The numbers on the plotting screen steadily worsened. Barometric pressure sank to 980, 975, 965 millibars. Wind velocity mounted to 75 knots, 95, 110. She was a full-grown hurricane by ten o'clock.

Ted leaned across his desk and tapped out a name for the storm on the viewscreen's keyboard: *Omega*.

"One way or the other, she's the end of THUNDER," he muttered.

The letters glowed out at the top of the plotting screen. Across the vast room, one of the girls broke into sobs.

Through the early hours of the morning, Hurricane

Omega grew steadily in size and strength. An immense band of clouds towered from the sea to some sixty thousand feet, pouring two inches of rain per hour over an area of nearly 300,000 square miles. The pressure at her core had plummeted to 950 millibars and central windspeeds were gusting to better than 140 knots, and still rising.

"It's almost as if she's alive," Tuli whispered as we watched the viewscreen. "She grows, she feeds, she moves."

By two A.M., Miami time, dawn was breaking over Hurricane Omega. Six trillion tons of air packing the energy of a hundred hydrogen bombs, a mammoth, mindless heat engine turned loose, aiming for civilization, for us.

Waves lashed by Omega's fury were spreading all across the Atlantic and would show up as dangerous surf on the beaches of four continents. Seabirds were sucked into the storm against their every exertion, to be drenched and battered to exhaustion; their only hope was to make it to the eye of the hurricane, where the air was calm and clear. A tramp steamer on the New York-to-Capetown run, five hundred miles from Omega's center, was calling frantically for help as mountainous waves overpowered the ship's puny pumps. Omega churned onward, releasing as much energy as a ten-megaton bomb every fifteen minutes.

We watched, we listened, fascinated. The face of our enemy, and it made all of us—even Ted, I think—feel completely helpless. At first Omega's eye, as seen from the satellite cameras, was vague and shifting, covered over by cirrus clouds. But finally it steadied and opened up, a strong column of clear air, the mighty central pillar of the hurricane, the pivotal anchor around which her furious winds wailed their primeval song of violence and terror.

Barney, Tuli, and I sat around Ted's desk, watching him;

his scowl deepened as the storm worsened. We didn't realize it was daylight until Dr. Weis phoned again. He looked haggard on the tiny desk-top viewscreen.

"I've been watching the storm all night," he said. "The President called me a few minutes ago and asked me what you were going to do about it."

Ted rubbed his eyes. "Can't knock her out, if that's what you mean. Too big now. Be like trying to stop a forest fire with a blanket."

"Well, you've got to do something!" Weis snapped. "All our reputations hang on that storm. Do you understand? Yours, mine, even the President's! To say nothing of the future for weather-control work in this country."

"Told you back in Washington last March," Ted countered, "that THUNDER was the wrong way to tackle hurricanes. . . ."

"Yes, and in July you announced to the press that no hurricanes would strike the United States! So now, instead of being an act of nature, hurricanes are a political issue."

Ted shook his head. "We've done the best we can."

"You've got to do more. You can try to steer the hurricane . . . change its path so that it won't strike the coast."

"You mean change the weather patterns?" Ted brightened. "Control the situation so that—"

"I do *not* mean weather control! Not over the United States," Dr. Weis said firmly. "But you can make whatever changes you have to over the ocean."

"That won't work," Ted answered. "Not enough leverage to do any good. Might budge her a few degrees, but she'll still wind up hitting the coast somewhere. All we'll be doing is fouling up the storm track so we won't know for sure where she'll hit."

"You've got to do something! We can't just sit here and let it happen to us. Ted, I haven't tried to tell you how to run THUNDER, but now I'm giving an order. You've got to make an attempt to steer the storm away from the coast. If we fail, at least we go down fighting. Maybe we can salvage something from this mess."

"Waste of time," Ted muttered.

Dr. Weis' shoulders moved as if he was wringing his hands, off camera. "Try it anyway. It might work. We might be lucky. . . ."

"Okay," Ted said, shrugging. "You're the boss."

The screen went dark. Ted looked up at us. "You heard the man. We're going to play Pied Piper."

"But we can't do it," Tuli said. "It can't be done."

"Doesn't matter. Weis is trying to save face. You ought to understand that, buddy."

Barney looked up at the plotting screen. Omega was northeast of Puerto Rico and boring in toward Florida.

"Why didn't you tell him the truth?" she asked Ted. "You know we can't steer Omega. Even if he'd let us try to control the weather completely, we couldn't be sure of keeping the storm off the coast. You shouldn't have——"

"Shouldn't have what?" Ted snapped back. "Shouldn't have taken THUNDER when Weis and the President offered it? Shouldn't have made that crack to the newsmen about stopping every hurricane? Shouldn't have told Weis we'd try to steer Omega? I did all three, and I'd do them all again. I'd rather do *something*, even if it's not the best something. Got to keep moving; once we stop, we're dead."

"But why," Barney asked, almost pleadingly, "did you make that insane promise to the newsmen?"

He frowned, but more at himself than at her. "How

should I know? Maybe because Weis was sitting there in front of the cameras looking so sure of himself. Safe and serene. Maybe I was crazy enough to think we could really sneak through a whole hurricane season okay. Maybe I'm just crazy, period. I don't know."

"But what do we do now?" I asked.

He cocked an eye at the plotting screen. "Try to steer Omega. Try saving Weis' precious face." Pointing to a symbol on the map several hundred miles north of the storm, he said, "There's a Navy sonar picket anchored out there. I'm going to buzz over to it, see if I can get a first-hand look at this monster."

"That's . . . that's dangerous," Barney said.

He shrugged.

"Ted, you can't run the operation from the middle of the ocean," I said.

"Picket's in a good spot to see the storm . . . at least the edge of it. Maybe I can wangle a plane ride through it. Been fighting hurricanes all season without seeing one. Besides, the ship's part of the Navy's antisubmarine warning net; loaded with communications gear. Be in touch with you every minute, don't worry."

"But if the storm comes that way . . ."

"Let it come," he said. "It's going to finish us anyway." He turned and strode off, leaving us to watch him.

Barney turned to me. "Jerry, he thinks we blame him for everything. We've got to stop him."

"No one can stop him. You know that. Once he gets his mind set on something. . . ."

"Then I'll go with him." She got up from her chair.

I took her arm.

"No, Jerry," she said, "I can't let him go alone."

"Is it the danger you're afraid of, or the fact that he's leaving?"

"Jerry, in the mood he's in now . . . he's reckless. . . ."

"All right," I said, trying to calm her. "All right. I'll go with him. I'll make sure he keeps his feet dry."

"But I don't want either one of you in danger!"

"I know. I'll take care of him."

She looked at me with those misty, gray-green eyes. "Jerry . . . you won't let him do anything foolish, will you?"

"You know me; I'm no hero."

"Yes, you are," she said. And I felt my insides do a handspring.

I left her there with Tuli and hurried out to the parking lot. The bright sunshine outdoors was a painful surprise. It was hot and muggy, even though the day was only an hour or so old.

Ted was getting into one of the Project staff cars when I caught up with him.

"A landlubber like you shouldn't be loose on the ocean by himself," I said.

He grinned. "Hop aboard, salt."

The day was sultry. The usual tempering sea breezes had died off. As we drove along the Miami bayfront, the air was oppressive, ominous. The sky was brazen, the water deathly calm. The old-timers along the fishing docks were squinting out at the horizon to the south and nodding to each other. It was coming.

The color of the sea, the shape of the clouds, the sighting of a shark near the coast, the way the seabirds were perching—all these became omens.

It was coming.

We slept for most of the flight out to the sonar picket.

The Navy jet landed smoothly in the softly billowing sea and a helicopter from the picket brought us aboard. The ship was similar in style to the deep-sea mining dredges of Thornton Pacific. For antisubmarine work, though, the dredging equipment was replaced by a fantastic array of radar and communications antennas.

"Below decks are out of bounds to visitors, I'm afraid," said the chunky lieutenant who welcomed us to his ship. As we walked from the helicopter landing pad on the fantail toward the bridge, he told us, "This bucket's a floating sonar station. Everything below decks is classified except the galley, and the cook won't let even me in there."

He laughed at his own joke. He was a pleasant-faced Yankee, about our own age, square-jawed, solidly built, the kind that stays in the Navy for life.

We clambered up a ladder to the bridge.

"We're anchored here," the lieutenant said, "with special bottom gear and arresting cables. So the bridge isn't used for navigation as much as for communications."

Looking around, we could see what he meant. The bridge's aft bulkhead was literally covered with viewscreens, autoplotters, and electronics controls.

"I think you'll be able to keep track of your hurricane without much trouble." He nodded proudly toward the communications equipment.

"If we can't," Ted said, "it won't be your fault."

The lieutenant introduced us to his chief communications technician, a scrappy little sailor who had just received his engineering degree and was putting in two Navy years. Within minutes we were talking to Tuli back in THUNDER headquarters.

"Omega seems to have slowed down quite a bit," Tuli

said, his impassive face framed by the viewscreen. "She's about halfway between your position and Puerto Rico."

"Gathering strength," Ted muttered.

They fed the information from THUNDER's computers to the picket's autoplotter, and soon we had a miniature version of Ted's giant map on one of the bridge's screens.

Ted studied the map, mumbling to himself. "If we could feed her some warm water . . . give her a shortcut to the outbound leg of the Gulf Stream . . . then maybe she'd bypass the coast."

The lieutenant was watching us from a jumpseat that folded out of the port bulkhead.

"Just wishful thinking," Ted muttered on. "Fastest way to move her is to set up a low-pressure cell to the north . . . make her swing more northerly. . . ."

He talked it over with Tuli for the better part of an hour, perching on a swivel stool set into the deck next to the chart table. The cook popped through the bridge's starboard hatch with a tray of sandwiches and coffee. Ted absently took a sandwich and mug, still locked in talk with Tuli.

Finally he said to the viewscreen image, "Okay, we deepen this trough off Long Island and try to make a real storm cell out of it."

Tuli nodded, but he was clearly unhappy.

"Get Barney to run it through the computer as fast as she can, but you'd better get the planes out right now. Don't wait for the computer run. Got to hit while she's still sitting around. Otherwise. . . ." His voice trailed off.

"All right," Tuli said. "But we're striking blindly."

"I know. Got any better ideas?"

Tuli shrugged.

"Then let's scramble the planes." He turned to me. "Jerry, we've got a battle plan figured out. Tuli'll give you the details."

Now it was my turn. I spent the better part of the afternoon getting the right planes with the right payloads off to the exact places where the work had to be done. Through it all, I was calling myself an idiot for tracking out to this mid-ocean exile. It took twice as long to process the orders as it would have back at headquarters.

"Don't bother saying it," Ted said when I finished. "So it was kinky coming out here. Okay. Just had to get away from that place before I went over the hill."

"But what good are you going to do here?" I asked.

He gripped the bridge's rail and looked out past the ship's prow, toward the horizon.

"We can run the show from here just as well . . . maybe a little tougher than back in Miami, but we can do it. If everything goes okay, we'll get brushed by the storm's edge. I'd like to see that. Want to feel her, see what she can do. Never seen a hurricane from this close. And it's better than sitting in that windowless cocoon back there."

"And if things don't go well?" I asked. "If the storm doesn't move the way you want it to?"

He turned away. "Probably she won't."

"Then we might miss the whole show."

"Maybe. Or she might march right down here and blow down our necks."

"Omega might . . . we could be caught in the middle of it?"

"Could be," he said easily. "Better get some sleep while you can. Going to be busy later on."

The exec showed us to a tiny stateroom with two bunks

in it. Part of the picket's crew was on shore leave, and they had a spare compartment for us. I tried to sleep, but spent most of the late-afternoon hours squirming uncomfortably. Around dusk, Ted got up and went to the bridge. I followed him.

"See those clouds, off the southern horizon," he was saying to the lieutenant. "That's her. Just the outer fringes."

I checked back with THUNDER headquarters. The planes had seeded the low-pressure trough off Long Island without incident. Weather stations along the coast, and automated equipment on satellites and planes, were reporting a small storm cell developing.

Barney's face appeared on the viewscreen. She looked very worried. "Is Ted there?"

"Right here." He stepped into view.

"The computer run just finished," she said, pushing a strand of hair from her face. "Omega's going to turn northward, but only temporarily. She'll head inland again early tomorrow. In about forty-eight hours she'll strike the coast somewhere between Cape Hatteras and Washington."

Ted let out a low whistle.

"But that's not all," she continued. "The storm track crosses right over the ship you're on. You're going to be in the center of it!"

"We'll have to get off here right away," I said.

"No rush," Ted replied. "We can spend the night here. I want to see her develop firsthand."

Barney said, "Ted, don't be foolish. It's going to be dangerous."

He grinned at her. "Jealous? Don't worry, I just want to get a look at her, then I'll come flying home to you."

"You stubborn. . . ." The blonde curl popped back over her eyes again and she pushed it away angrily. "Ted, it's time you stopped acting like a spoiled little boy! You bet I'm jealous. I'm tired of competing against the whole twirling atmosphere! You've got responsibilities, and if you don't want to live up to them . . . well, you'd better, that's all!"

"Okay, okay. We'll be back tomorrow morning. Be safer traveling in daylight anyway. Omega's still moving slowly; we'll have plenty time."

"Not if she starts to move faster. This computer run was only a first-order look at the problem. The storm could accelerate sooner than we think."

"We'll get to Miami okay, don't worry."

"No, why should I worry?" Barney said. "You're only six hundred miles out at sea with a hurricane bearing down on you."

"Just an hour away from home. Get some sleep. We'll fly over in the morning."

The wind was picking up as I went back to my bunk, and the ship was starting to rock in the deepening sea. I had sailed open boats through storms and slept in worse weather than this. It wasn't the conditions of the moment that bothered me. It was the knowledge of what was coming.

Ted stayed out on deck, watching the southern skies darken with the deathly fascination of a general observing the approach of a much stronger army. I dropped off to sleep telling myself that I'd get Ted off this ship as soon as a plane could pick us up, even if I had to get the sailors to wrap him in anchor chains.

By morning, it was raining hard and the ship was bucking badly in the heavy waves. It was an effort to push through the narrow passageway to the bridge, with the deck bobbing beneath my feet and the ship tossing hard enough to slam me against the bulkheads.

Up on the bridge, the wind was howling evilly as a sailor helped me into a slicker and life vest. When I turned to tug them on, I saw that the helicopter pad out on the stern was empty.

"Chopper took most of the crew out about an hour ago," the sailor hollered into my ear. "Went to meet the sea-plane west of here, where it ain't so rough. When it comes back we're all pulling out."

I nodded and thanked him.

"She's a beauty, isn't she?" Ted shouted at me as I stepped onto the open section of the bridge. "Moving up a lot faster than we thought."

I grabbed a handhold between him and the lieutenant. To the south of us was a solid wall of black. Waves were breaking over the bows and the rain was a battering force against our faces.

"Will the helicopter be able to get back to us?" I asked the lieutenant.

"We've had worse blows than this," he shouted back, "but I wouldn't want to hang around for another hour or so."

The communications tech staggered across the bridge to us. "Chopper's on the way, sir. Ought to be here in ten to fifteen minutes."

The lieutenant nodded. "I'll have to go aft and see that

the helicopter's properly dogged down when she lands. You two be ready to hop on when the word goes out."

"We'll be ready," I said.

As the lieutenant left the bridge, I asked Ted, "Well, is this doing you any good? Frankly, I would've been a lot happier in Miami. . . ."

"She's a real brute," he shouted. "This is a lot different from watching a map."

"But why. . . ."

"This is the enemy, Jerry. This is what we're trying to kill. Think how much better you're going to feel after we've learned how to stop hurricanes."

"If we live long enough to learn how!"

The helicopter struggled into view, leaning heavily into the raging wind. I watched, equally fascinated and terrified, as it worked its way to the landing pad, tried to come down, got blown backwards by a terrific gust, fought toward the pad again, and finally touched down on the heaving deck. A team of sailors scrambled across the wet square to attach heavy lines to the landing gear, even before the rotor blades started to slow down. A wave smashed across the ship's stern and one of the sailors went sprawling. Only then did I notice that each man had a stout lifeline around his middle. They finally got the 'copter secured.

I turned back to Ted. "Let's go before it's too late."

We started down the slippery ladder to the main deck. As we inched back toward the stern, a tremendous wave caught the picket amidships and sloughed her around broadside. The little ship shuddered violently and the deck dropped out from under us. I sagged to my knees.

Ted pulled me up. "Come on, buddy, Omega's here."

Another wave smashed across us. I grabbed for a hand-hold and as my eyes cleared, saw the helicopter pitching crazily over to one side, the moorings on her landing gear flapping loosely in the wind.

"It's broken away!"

The deck heaved again and the 'copter careened over on its side, rotors smashing against the pad. Another wave caught us. The ship bucked terribly. The helicopter slid backwards along its side and then, lifted by a solid wall of foaming green, smashed through the gunwale and into the sea.

Groping senselessly on my hands and knees, soaking wet, battered like an overmatched prizefighter, I watched our only link to safety disappear into the furious sea.

19. The Weathermakers

∧∧∨∧∨∧∨∧∨∧∨∧∨∧∨∧∨∧∨∧∨

I CLAMBERED to my feet on the slippery deck of the Navy picket. The ship shuddered again and slewed around. A wave hit the other side and washed across, putting us knee-deep in foaming water until the deck lurched upward again and cleared the waves temporarily.

"Omega's won," Ted roared in my ear, over the screaming wind. "We're trapped!"

We stood there, hanging onto the handholds. The sea was impossible to describe—a tangled fury of waves, with no sense or pattern to them, their tops ripped off by the wind, spray mixing with blinding rain.

The lieutenant groped by, edging hand-over-hand on the lifeline that ran along the superstructure bulkhead.

"Are you two all right?"

"No broken bones."

"You'd better come up to the bridge," he shouted. We were face-to-face, nearly touching noses, yet we could hardly hear him. "I've given orders to cast off the anchors and get up steam. We've got to try to ride out this blow under power. If we just sit here we'll be swamped."

"Is there anything we can do?"

He shot me a grim look. "Next time you tinker with a hurricane, make it when I'm on shore!"

We followed the lieutenant up to the bridge. I nearly fell off the rain-slicked ladder, but Ted grabbed me with one of his powerful paws.

The bridge was sloshing from the monstrous waves and spray that were drenching the decks. The communications panels seemed to be intact, though. We could see the map that Ted had set up on the autoplotter screen; it was still alight. Omega spread across the screen like an engulfing demon. The tiny pinpoint of light marking the ship's location was well inside the hurricane's swirl.

The lieutenant fought his way to the ship's intercom while Ted and I grabbed for handholds.

"All the horses you've got, Chief," I heard the lieutenant bellow into the intercom mike. "I'll get every available man on the pumps. Keep those engines going. If we lose power we're sunk!"

I realized he meant it literally.

The lieutenant crossed over toward us and hung on to the chart table.

"Is that map accurate?" he yelled at Ted.

The big redhead nodded. "Up to the minute. Why?"

"I'm trying to figure a course that'll take us out of this blow. We can't stand much more of this battering. She's taking on more water than the pumps can handle. Engine room's getting swamped."

"Head southwest then," Ted said at the top of his lungs. "Get out of her quickest that way."

"We can't! I've got to keep the sea on our bows or else we'll capsize!"

"What?"

"He's got to point her into the wind," I yelled. "Just about straight into the waves."

"Right!" the lieutenant agreed.

"But you'll be riding along with the storm. Never get out that way. She'll just carry us along all day!"

"How do you know which way the storm's going to go? She might change course."

"Not a chance." Ted jabbed a finger toward the plotting screen. "She's heading northwesterly now and she'll stay on that course the rest of the day. Best bet is to head for the eye."

"Toward the center? We'd never make it!"

Ted shook his head. "Never get out of it if you keep heading straight into the wind. But if you can make five knots or so, we can spiral into the eye. Calm there."

The lieutenant stared at the screen. "Are you sure? Do you know exactly where the storm's moving and how fast she's going to go?"

"We can check it out."

Quickly, we called THUNDER headquarters, transmitting up to the Atlantic Station satellite for relay to Miami. Barney was nearly frantic, but we got her off the line fast. Tuli answered our questions and gave us the exact predictions for Omega's direction and speed.

Ted went inside with a soggy handful of notes to put the information into the ship's course computer. Barney pushed her way onto the viewscreen.

"Jerry . . . are you all right?"

"I've been better, but we'll get through it okay. The ship's in no real trouble," I lied.

"You're sure?"

"Certainly. Ted's working out a course with the skipper. We'll be back in Miami in a few hours."

"It looks awful out there."

Another mammoth wave broke across the bow and drowned the bridge with spray.

"It's not picnic weather," I admitted, "but we're not worried, so don't you go getting upset." *Not worried*, I added silently, *we're scared white*.

Reluctantly, the lieutenant agreed to head for the storm's eye. It was either that or face a battering that would split the ship in a few hours. We told Tuli to send a plane to the eye to try to pick us up.

Time lost all meaning. We just hung on, drenched to the skin, plunging through a wild, watery inferno, the wind shrieking evilly at us, the seas absolutely chaotic. No one remained on the bridge except the lieutenant, Ted, and me. The rest of the ship's skeleton crew were below decks, working every pump on board as hard as they could be run. The ship's autopilot and computer-run guidance system kept us heading on the course Ted and the lieutenant had figured.

Passing into the hurricane's eye was like stepping through a door from bedlam to a peaceful garden. One minute we were being pounded by mountainous waves and merciless wind, with rain and spray making it hard to see even the bow. Then the sun broke through and the wind abruptly died. The waves were still hectic, frothing, as we limped out into the open. But at least we could raise our heads without being battered by the wind-driven spray.

Towering clouds rose all about us, but this patch of ocean was safe. Birds hovered around us, and high overhead a vertijet was circling, sent out by Tuli. The plane made a tight pass over us, then descended onto the helicopter landing pad on the ship's fantail. Her landing gear barely touched the deck, and her tail stuck out over the smashed railing where the helicopter had broken through.

We had to duck under the plane's nose and enter from a hatch in her belly because the outer wing jets were still blazing. As we huddled in the crammed passenger compartment, the plane hoisted straight up. The jetpods swiveled back for horizontal flight and the wings slid to supersonic sweep. We climbed steeply and headed up over the clouds.

As I looked down at the fast-shrinking little picket, I realized the lieutenant was also craning his neck at the port for a last look.

"I'm sorry you had to lose your ship," I said.

"Well, another hour in those seas would have finished us," he said quietly. But he kept staring wistfully out the port until the clouds covered the abandoned vessel.

Barney was waiting for us at the Navy airport with dry clothes, the latest charts and forecasts on Omega, and a large share of feminine emotion. I'll never forget the sight of her running toward us as we stepped down from the vertijet's main hatch. She threw her arms around Ted's neck, then around mine, and then around Ted again.

"You had me so frightened, the two of you!"

Ted laughed. "We were kind of ruffled ourselves."

It took nearly an hour to get away from the airport. Navy brass hats, debriefing officers, newsmen, photographers— they all wanted a crack at us. I turned them onto the lieutenant: "He's the real hero," I told them. "Without him, we would've all drowned." While they converged on him,

Ted and I got a chance to change our clothes in an officers' wardroom and scuttle out to the car Barney had waiting.

"Dr. Weis has been on the phone all day," Barney said as the driver pulled out for the main highway leading to the Miami bayfront and THUNDER headquarters.

Ted frowned and spread the reports on Omega across his lap.

Sitting between the two of us, she pointed to the latest chart. "Here's the storm track . . . ninety percent reliability, plus-or-minus two percent."

Ted whistled. "Right smack into Washington and then up the coast. She's going to damage more than reputations."

"I told Dr. Weis you'd call his as soon as you could."

"Okay," he said reluctantly. "Let's get it over with."

I punched out the Science Adviser's private number on the phone set into the car's seat. After a brief word with a secretary, Dr. Weis' drawn face appeared on the viewscreen.

"You're safe," he said bleakly.

"Disappointed?"

"The way this hurricane is coming at us, we could use a martyr or two."

"Steering didn't work," Ted said. "Only thing left to try is what we should've done in the first place. . . ."

"Weather control? Absolutely not! Being hit with a hurricane is bad enough, but if you try tinkering with the weather all across the country, we'll have every farmer, every vacationist, every mayor and governor and traffic cop on our necks!"

Ted fumed. "What else are you going to do? Sit there

and take it? Weather control's the last chance of stopping this beast. . . ."

"Marrett, I'm almost ready to believe that you set up this storm purposely to force us into letting you try your pet idea!"

"If I could do that, I wouldn't be sitting here arguing with you."

"Possibly not. But you listen to me. Weather control is out. If we have to take a hurricane, that's what we'll do. We'll have to admit that THUNDER was too ambitious a project for the first time around. We'll have to back off. We'll try something like THUNDER again next year, but without all the fanfare. You'll have to lead a very quiet life for a few years, Marrett, but at least we might be able to keep going."

"Why back down when you can go ahead and stop this hurricane?" Ted argued. "We can push Omega out to sea, I know we can!"

"The way you steered her? That certainly boomeranged on you."

"We tried moving six trillion tons of air with a feather-duster! I'm talking about real control of the weather patterns across the whole continent. It'll work!"

"You can't guarantee that it will, and even if you did I wouldn't believe you. Marrett, I want you to go back to THUNDER headquarters and sit there quietly. You may operate on any new disturbances that show up. But you are to leave Omega strictly alone. Is that clear? If you try to touch that storm in any way, I'll see to it that you're finished. For good."

Dr. Weis snapped off the connection. The viewscreen

went dark, almost as dark as the scowl on Ted's face. For the rest of the ride back to Project headquarters he said nothing. He simply sat there, slouched over, pulled in on himself, his eyes smoldering.

When the car stopped he looked up at us.

"What'd you do if I gave the word to push Omega off the coast?"

"But Dr. Weis said. . . ."

"I don't care what he said, or what he does afterward. We can stop Omega."

Barney turned and looked at me.

"Ted—I can always go back to Hawaii and help my Father make his twentieth million. But what about you? Weis can finish your career permanently. And what about Barney and the rest of the Project personnel?"

"It's my responsibility. Weis won't care about the rest of 'em. And I don't care what he does to me. . . . I can't sit here like a dumb ape and let that hurricane have its own way. Got a score to settle with Omega."

"Regardless of what it'll cost you?"

He nodded gravely. "Regardless of everything. Are you with me?"

"I guess I'm as crazy as you are," I heard myself say. "Let's do it."

We piled out of the car and strode up to the control center. As people started to cluster around us, Ted raised his arms for silence:

"Now listen—Project THUNDER is dead. We've got a job of weathermaking to do. We're going to push that hurricane out to sea."

Then he started rattling off orders as though he had been rehearsing for this moment all his life.

As I started for my cubicle, Barney touched my sleeve. "Jerry, whatever happens later, thanks for helping him."

"We're accomplices," I said. "Before, during, and after the fact."

She smiled. "Do you think you could ever look at a cloud in the sky again if you hadn't agreed to help him try this?"

Before I could think of a reply she turned and started toward the computer section.

We had roughly thirty-six hours before Omega would strike the Virginia coast and then head up Chesapeake Bay for Washington. Thirty-six hours to manipulate the weather over the entire North American continent.

Within three hours Ted had us around his desk, a thick wad of notes clenched in his right hand. "Not as bad as it could've been," he told us, gesturing toward the plotting screen. "This big High sitting near the Great Lakes—good cold, dry air that can make a shield over the East Coast if we can swing it into position. Tuli, that's your job."

Tuli nodded, bright-eyed with excitement.

"Barney, we'll need pinpoint forecasts for every part of the country, even if it takes every computer in the Weather Bureau to wring 'em out."

"Right, Ted."

"Jerry, communications are the key. Got to keep in touch with the whole blinking country. And we're going to need planes, rockets, even slingshots maybe. Get the ball rolling before Weis finds out what we're up to."

"What about the Canadians? You'll be affecting their weather too."

"Get that liaison guy from the State Department and tell him to have the Canadian weather bureau check with us. Don't spill the beans to him, though."

"It's only a matter of time until Washington catches on," I said.

"Most of what we've got to do has to be done tonight. By the time they wake up tomorrow, we'll be on our way."

Omega's central windspeeds had climbed to 120 knots by evening, and were still increasing. As she trundled along toward the coast, her howling fury was nearly matched by the uproar of action at our control center. We didn't eat, we didn't sleep. We worked!

A half-dozen military satellites armed with lasers started pumping streams of energy into areas pinpointed by Ted's orders. Their crews had been alerted weeks earlier to co-operate with requests from Project THUNDER, and Ted and others from our technical staff had briefed them before the hurricane season began. They didn't question our messages. Squadrons of planes flew out to dump chemicals and seeding materials off Long Island, where he had created a weak storm cell in the vain attempt to steer Omega. Ted wanted that Low deepened, intensified—a low-pressure trough into which that High on the Great Lakes could slide.

"Intensifying the Low will let Omega come in faster, too," Tuli pointed out.

"Know it," Ted answered. "But the numbers're on our side. I think. Besides, faster Omega moves, less chance she gets to build up higher wind velocities."

By ten P.M. we had asked for and received a special analysis from the National Meteorological Center in Maryland. It showed that we would have to deflect the jet stream slightly, since it controlled the upper-air flow patterns across the country. But how do you divert a river that's three hundred miles wide, four miles thick, and racing along at better than three hundred miles per hour?

"It would take a hundred-megaton bomb," Barney said, "exploded about fifteen miles over Salt Lake City."

Ted nearly laughed. "The UN'd need a year just to get it on their agenda. Not to mention the sovereign citizens of Utah and points east."

"Then how do we do it?"

Ted grabbed the coffeepot standing on his desk and poured himself a mug of steaming black liquid. "Jet stream's a shear layer between the polar and mid-latitude tropopauses," he muttered, more to himself than any of us. "If you reinforce the polar air, it can nudge the stream southward. . . ."

He took a cautious sip of the hot coffee. "Tuli, we're already moving a High southward from the Great Lakes. How about moving a bigger polar mass from Canada to push the jet stream enough to help us?"

"We don't have enough time or equipment to operate in Canada," I said. "And we'd need permission from Ottawa."

"What about reversing the procedure?" Tuli asked. "We could shrink the desert High over Arizona and New Mexico slightly, and the jet stream will move southward."

Ted hiked his eyebrows. "Think you can do it?"

"I'll have to make a few calculations."

"Okay, scramble."

The next morning in Boston, people who had gone to bed with a weather forecast of "warm, partly cloudy," awoke to a chilly, driving northeast rain. The Low we had intensified during the night had surprised the local fore-casters. The Boston Weather Bureau office issued corrected predictions through the morning as the little rainstorm moved out, the Great Lakes High slid in and caused a flurry of frontal squalls, and finally the sun broke through. The cool dry air of the High dropped local temperatures more than ten degrees within an hour. To the unknowing New Englanders it was just another day, merely slightly more bewildering than most.

Dr. Weis phoned at seven thirty that morning.

"Marrett, have you lost your mind? What do you think you're doing? I told you. . . ."

"Can't chat now, we're busy," Ted shot back.

"I'll have your hide for this!"

"Tomorrow you can have my hide. Bring it up myself. But first I'm going to find out if I'm right or wrong about this."

The Science Adviser turned purple. "I'm going to send out an order to all Government installations to stop . . ."

"Better not. We're right in the middle of some tricky moves. Besides, we'll never find out if it works or not. Most of the mods've been made. Let's see what good they do."

Barney rushed up with a ream of computer print-out sheets as Ted cut the phone connection.

"There's going to be a freeze in the Central Plains and northern Rockies," she said, pushing back her tousled hair. "There'll be some snow. We haven't fixed the exact amount yet."

A harvest-time freeze. Crops ruined, cities paralyzed by unexpected snow, weekend holidays ruined, and in the mountains deaths from exertion and exposure.

"Get the forecast out on the main Weather Bureau network," Ted ordered. "Warn 'em fast."

The plotting screen showed our battle clearly. Omega, with central wind speeds of 175 knots now, was still pushing toward Virginia. But her forward progress was slowing, ever so slightly, as the Great Lakes High moved southeastward past Pittsburgh.

By noontime Ted was staring at the screen and muttering, "Won't be enough. Not unless the jet stream comes around a couple of degrees."

It was raining in Washington now, and snow was starting to fall in Winnipeg. I was trying to handle three phone calls at once when I heard an ear-splitting whoop from Ted. I looked toward the plotting screen. There was a slight bend in the jet stream west of the Mississippi that hadn't been there before.

As soon as I could, I collared Tuli for an explanation.

"We used the lasers from the Atlantic Station and every ounce of catalysts I could find. The effect isn't spectacular, no noticeable weather change. But the desert High has shrunk slightly and the jet stream has moved a little southward, temporarily."

"Will it be enough?" I asked.

He shrugged.

Through the long afternoon we watched that little curl travel along the length of the jet stream's course, like a wave snaking down the length of a long, taut rope. Meanwhile the former Great Lakes High was covering all of Maryland and pushing into Virginia. Its northern extension shielded the coast well into New England.

"But she'll blast right through," Ted grumbled, watching Omega's glowering system of closely packed isobars, "unless the jet stream helps push her off."

I asked Barney, "How does the timing look? Which will arrive first, the jet-stream change or the storm?"

She shook her head. "The machines have taken it down to four decimal places and there's still no sure answer."

Norfolk was being drenched by a torrential downpour; gale-force winds were snapping power lines and knocking down trees. Washington was a darkened, wind-swept city. Most of the Federal offices had closed early, and traffic was inching along the rain-slicked streets.

Boatmen from Hatteras to the fishhook angle of Cape Cod—weekend sailors and professionals alike—were making fast extra lines, setting out double anchors, or pulling their craft out of the water altogether. Commercial airlines were juggling their schedules around the storm and whole squadrons of military planes were winging westward, away from the danger, like great flocks of migrating birds.

Storm tides were piling up all along the coast, and flood warnings were flashing from civil defense centers in a dozen states. The highways were filling with people moving inland before the approaching fury.

And Omega was still a hundred miles out to sea.

Then she faltered.

You could feel the electricity crackle through our control center. The mammoth hurricane hovered off the coast as the jet-stream deflection finally arrived. We all held our breaths. Omega stood off the coast uncertainly for an endless hour, then turned to the northeast. She began to head out to sea.

We shouted our foolish heads off.

When the furor died down, Ted hopped up on his desk. "Hold it, heroes! Job's not finished yet. We've got a freeze in the Midwest to modify, and I want to throw everything we've got into Omega, weaken the old girl as much as possible. Now *scramble!*"

It was nearly midnight before Ted let us call it quits. Our Project people—real weathermakers now—had weakened Omega to the point where she was only a tropical storm, fast losing her punch over the cold waters of the north Atlantic. A light snow was sprinkling parts of the Upper Midwest, but our warning forecasts had been in time, and the weathermakers were able to take most of the snap out of the cold front. The local weather stations were reporting only minor problems from the freeze. The snow amounted to less than an inch.

Most of the Project people had left for sleep. There was only a skeleton crew left in the control center. Barney, Tuli, and I gravitated toward Ted's desk. He had commandeered a typewriter and was pecking on the keys.

"How do you spell 'resignation'?" he asked.

Before any of us could answer, the phone buzzed. Ted thumbed the "on" switch. It was Dr. Weis.

"You didn't have to call," Ted said. "Game's over. I know it."

Dr. Weis looked utterly exhausted, as if he had personally been battling the storm. "I had a long talk with the President tonight, Marrett. You've put him in a difficult position, and me in an impossible one. To the general public, you're a hero. But I wouldn't trust you as far as I could throw a cyclotron."

"Don't blame you, I guess," Ted answered calmly. "But

don't worry, you won't have to fire me. I'm resigning. You'll be off the hook."

"You can't quit," Dr. Weis said bitterly. "You're a national resource, as far as the President's concerned. He spent the night comparing you to nuclear energy: he wants you tamed and harnessed."

"Harnessed? For weather control?"

Weis nodded wordlessly.

"The President wants to really work on weather control?" Ted broke into a huge grin. "That's a harness I've been trying to get into for four years."

"Listen to me, Marrett. The President wants you to work on weather control, but I'm the one who's going to be responsible for controlling you. And I will never—do you hear, *never*—allow you to direct a project or get anywhere near directing a project. I'm going to find bosses for you who can keep you bottled up tight. We'll do weather-control work, and we'll use your ideas. But you'll never be in charge of anything as long as I'm in Washington."

Ted's smile died. "Okay," he said grimly, "as long as the work gets done . . . and done right. I didn't expect to get a National Medal out of this anyway."

Still glaring, Dr. Weis said, "You were lucky, Marrett. Very lucky. If the weather patterns had been slightly different, if things hadn't worked out so well. . . ."

"Wasn't luck," Ted flashed. "It was work, a lot of peoples' work, and brains and guts. That's where weather control— *real* weather control—wins for you. It doesn't matter what the weather patterns are if you're going to change 'em all to suit your needs. You don't need luck, just time and sweat. You *make* the weather you want. That's what we did. That's why it had to work; we just had to tackle it on a big-enough scale."

"Luck or skill," Dr. Weis said wearily, "it doesn't matter. You'll get weather control now. But under my direction, and on my terms."

"We've won," Ted said as he shut off the phone. "We've really won."

Barney sank into the nearest chair. "It's too much happening all at once. I don't think I can believe it all."

"It's real," Ted answered quietly. "Weather control is a fact now. We're going to do it."

"You'll have to work under Dr. Weis and whoever he appoints to handle the program," I said.

Ted shrugged. "I worked for Rossman. I can work for anybody. The work's important, not the titles they give you."

Tuli rubbed his midsection and said, "I don't know about you inscrutable westerners, but this red-blooded Mongol is starving."

"So'm I, come to think of it," Ted said. "Come on you guys, let's have a celebration breakfast!"

"Guys," Barney echoed, frowning.

"Hey, that's right, you're a girl. Come on, Girl. Looks like you won't have to play second fiddle to hurricanes any more." He took her arm and started for the door. "Think you can stand being the center of my attention?"

Barney looked back at me. I got up and took her other arm. "If you don't mind, she's going to be the center of my attention, too."

Tuli shook his head as he joined us. "You barbarians. No wonder you're nervous wrecks. You never know who's going to marry whom. I've got my future wife all picked out; our families agreed on the match when we were both four years old."

"That's why you're here in the States," Ted joked.

Barney said, "Tuli, don't do anything to make them change their minds. I haven't had this much attention since *I* was four."

Down the main stairway we went, and out onto the street. The sidewalks were puddled from rain, a side effect of Omega, but overhead the stars were shining through tattered, scudding clouds.

"Today the world's going to wake up and discover that man can control the weather," Ted said.

"Not really," Tuli cautioned. "We've only made a beginning. We still have years of learning ahead. Decades, perhaps centuries."

Ted nodded, a contented smile on his face. "Maybe. But we've started. That's the important thing."

"And the political problems this is going to cause?" I asked. "The social and economic changes that weather control will bring? What about them?"

He laughed. "That's for administrators like you and the President to worry about. I've got enough to keep me busy: six quadrillion tons of air . . . and one mathematician."

Epilogue

A LITTLE more than two years later, on a golden October afternoon, the United Nations convened a special outdoor session in Washington to hear an address by the President.

It was the first time I had seen Barney and Ted since their wedding, six months earlier. She had told me about her decision as gently as possible, and I learned that it's possible to live with pain even if there's no hope that it will ever be completely cured.

I had been running Aeolus; there was plenty of work for the Laboratory now. Ted and Barney (and Tuli, too) were living in Washington and working on the Government's weather-control program. Ted had settled down, under the direction of one of the nation's top scientists, and was seeing our years of struggle turned into solid accomplishment.

The UN delegates met at a special outdoor pavilion, built along the banks of the Potomac for their ceremony. Key people from the Weather Bureau and Congress and Government were in the audience. Beyond the seats set on the grass for the delegates and invited guests, a huge thronging crowd looked on, and listened to the President.

". . . For mankind's technology," he was saying, "is both a constant danger and a constant opportunity. Through technology, man has attained the power to destroy himself, or the power to unite this planet in peace and freedom—freedom from war, from hunger, and from ignorance.

"Today we meet to mark a new step in the peaceful use of man's growing technical knowledge: the establishment of the United Nations Commission for Planetary Weather Control. . . ."

Like Ted's victory over Hurricane Omega, this was only a first step. Total control of the weather, and total solution of the human problems involved, was still a long way off. But we were started along the right road.

In my jacket pocket was a letter from the UN Secretary-General asking me to serve on the staff of the Planetary Weather Control Commission. I knew that Ted had a similar letter, and that Tuli would be getting one soon.

As we sat together listening to the President, a gentle breeze wafted by, tossing the flame-colored trees and tempering the warmth of the sun. It was a fine, crisp autumn afternoon: bright blue sky, beaming sun, occasional puffs of cotton-ball cumulus clouds. A perfect day for an outdoor ceremony.

Of course.

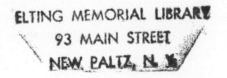
ELTING MEMORIAL LIBRARY
93 MAIN STREET
NEW PALTZ, N. Y.

ABOUT THE AUTHOR

BEN BOVA, whose work as a marketing co-ordinator for the Avco Everett Research Laboratory involves him in many aspects of technical communications, studied journalism at Temple University. After receiving his BS degree, he became a technical editor on Project Vanguard at the Martin Company and later wrote motion picture scripts for the Physical Science Study Committee (now Educational Services, Inc.), Watertown, Massachusetts.

A member of the National Association of Science Writers, a charter member of the Science Fiction Writers of America, and a member of the American Association for the Advancement of Science, Mr. Bova is the author of many books and articles on various scientific subjects.

Author of *The Uses of Space* and two other science fiction books for young people, *Star Watchman* and *The Star Conquerors*, he explained how this book came about: "Once we were planning to leave for a motor trip cross-country and got hit by a snowstorm. The Weather Bureau predicted that the snow would stop at 9 A.M. Precisely at 9, I went outside. The snow had just stopped, clouds were moving off, and blue sky was visible. Suppose we could have that accuracy all the time, I wondered. Better yet, *suppose we could make it happen?* Thus THE WEATHERMAKERS."